The Ugly Stepsister

The Ugly Stepsister

Avril Sabine

Cracked Acorn Productions
Australia

The Ugly Stepsister

Published by

Cracked Acorn Productions

PO Box 1365

Gympie, Queensland 4570

Australia

978-1-925131-17-8 (Kindle)

978-1-925617-52-8 (EPUB)

978-1-925131-33-8 (Print)

Genre: Young Adult Contemporary Romance

Cover design by Caitlyn Petersen

For my own stepfather, who thankfully, was not the stereotypical wicked stepparent and welcomed us into his family.

Ellie likes her life just the way it is. So it's not perfect. Whose life is? Not to mention she could easily name a dozen girls from her school that would love to swap places with her. But then, they don't know her carefully guarded secret and she's going to make certain they never do.

*

This story was written by an Australian author
using Australian spelling.

Chapter One

Ellie leaned close to the mirror as she reapplied her lipstick, the sound of music barely muted by the bathroom door. Once the lipstick was capped she dropped it into her makeup bag and critically surveyed her face. Her silvery blue eye shadow was several shades lighter than her blue eyes, her long gold fringe curved across her right cheek and was pushed behind her ear on the left. She added more mascara and leaned back, smiling in satisfaction. Perfect. He wasn't about to say no. Although with the amount of alcohol she'd encouraged him to drink 'no' had probably been removed from his vocabulary.

Once again she pushed aside her doubts. What choice did she have? She shuddered when she thought of the past two weekends. None. Absolutely none.

After she shoved her makeup bag inside her

oversized, fake leather handbag, she straightened her short black dress and slung her bag on so the strap crossed her chest. Her mobile phone beeped and she pulled it out of the small zip up pocket on the outside of her handbag and read the message.

He's leaving. Front door. Will stall. Hurry.

Ellie swore when she read the message from Lauren, returned her phone to its pocket and unlocked the bathroom door. The sounds of the party rushed in around her and she nearly stumbled over the handful of people waiting to use the bathroom. Pushing through the crowd, she spotted Lauren near the front door. She wore a similar black dress to Ellie's and had a mixture of black and white chunky plastic bracelets on her wrists. Her hair was dark brown with white-blond streaks through it that made the brown look black in comparison. Around her neck she wore three bead necklaces made entirely of large white beads, each strand larger than the last.

Lauren spotted Ellie and grinned, waving her over. Her other hand clutched the arm of a boy with curly brown hair who looked barely thirteen. Ellie knew he was sixteen. He went to the same school as her and Lauren.

"Sam's about to go. He's already called a taxi," Lauren said.

"You weren't going to leave without me, were you?" Ellie linked her arm through Sam's. Although they were in the same grade, they weren't in any classes together. Nor had she spoken to him before today. The few times she'd seen Sam had been during the lunch hour when she was in the library, frantically doing last minute research for an assignment.

"N… no." Sam shook his head and stumbled with the sudden movement.

Lauren and Ellie's gazes met and they smiled. Ellie was starting to believe that this weekend might be different from the last two. When someone bumped into her, Ellie turned with a glare. It was another boy from school. "Watch it, David."

"Ell–ieeee!" David's words were a little slurred as he draped an arm around her shoulders, drawing her name out. "How've you been?" He noticed Sam and peered closer at him. "Hey, what're you doing with Baby Face? You're not going home with him are you? Don't tell me you're that desperate."

"How about I give you a call if I ever get desperate." Ellie grinned as she shrugged David's arm off. Maybe she'd got her hopes up too soon. She refused to let her smile falter even though she was mentally begging David not to ask her more questions.

David laughed. "I might be about." He turned when someone called his name. "See you at school Monday." He waved over his shoulder as he wandered off.

Relieved, Ellie turned back to Lauren. "I'll let you know where he lives when I get there." She glanced towards Sam.

Lauren threw an arm around her. "Take care. I wish my mum wasn't such a bitch. It's so unfair that I'm not allowed to have you over ever again."

"Don't worry about it. At least we had fun before we were caught." Lauren's mum had been livid. She'd never seen her that angry before. Yet another memory she pushed away, determined not to focus on it.

Lauren giggled. "Yeah, we did." She paused to listen. "Hey. My song. Take care." She waved before she disappeared into the crowd, her plastic bracelets bouncing.

Ellie frowned at Sam who swayed beside her. She guessed they should head outside before the taxi arrived and thought they no longer needed a lift. Sam willingly let her lead him out of the crowded house, stumbling several times. Ellie wondered if she'd encouraged him to drink too much. She pushed that thought aside. His problem if he didn't have the backbone to say no. She'd just have to keep an eye on him so she could move out of the way if he was going to be sick. Guilt tried to creep back in. She refused to allow it. It wasn't like she was hurting him. So maybe he'd have a headache in the morning, but that'd pass.

The taxi pulled up and she pushed aside her worries, helping Sam into the backseat. She nudged him. "What's your address?"

It took Sam several attempts to get the words out. The taxi driver pulled out onto the road with a shake of his head. Ellie bit back a smile at his expression. Sam slumped beside her, half asleep. She sighed heavily. Up until three weeks ago her weekends had been different. She'd spent every weekend at Lauren's house for the past two years, probably longer. She wasn't exactly sure when the ritual had started. Everything had changed when Lauren's mum had caught them sneaking back into the house after going to a party she'd said they couldn't go to. It hadn't been fair for her to say no. She just hadn't understood that everyone would be at the party. And that they'd had to go.

Now she thought Ellie was a bad influence and Lauren wasn't allowed to have anything to do with her. Luckily Lauren didn't agree. She didn't know what she'd do without her best friend. Ellie yawned, hoping it wouldn't be too much longer before they reached Sam's house. She didn't have a clue where it was.

The taxi finally pulled up and Ellie peered out the window. They were parked in front of a house that still had the outside light on. The neighbours' houses were completely dark. A short verandah protected the front door, one side of the verandah interrupted by a room that jutted out level with it and on the other a double garage. The front yard had several shady trees, tidy shrubs and immaculate flowerbeds. To the right of the garage was a two metre high wooden fence with a gate.

Ellie nudged Sam when the taxi driver told her the cost of the ride.

"Huh?" Sam squinted at her.

"You're home. Driver's waiting to be paid." Ellie nodded towards the front of the taxi.

"Hmm." Sam struggled to pull his wallet out of a pocket of his jeans.

Ellie took the wallet from him, paid the driver and helped Sam out of the taxi. She staggered as he stumbled against her, then tried to lead him to the front door. Sam pulled away, shaking his head. If Ellie hadn't caught him, he would have ended up sitting on the concrete driveway.

Maybe this hadn't been the best idea. "What are you trying to do, Sam?"

Sam pointed to the wooden fence. "Th… that…"

"Okay," Ellie interrupted. She didn't want to spend all night waiting for him to get an entire sentence out. She sighed. It wasn't really Sam that she was annoyed with. It was the entire situation.

Helping him to the gate, she slipped her hand inside the waist high circle, cut in the timber, to slide back the bolt. While she closed the gate, Sam staggered down the flight of concrete steps. They ended at a timber door set in a lower level of the house. When she joined him, his head rested against the door and his eyes were closed. He hadn't gone to sleep had he? She hoped not. She carefully shook his shoulder, worried he might fall over.

"Huh? Wha?" Sam looked around blearily.

"Key?"

"Ohh." Sam reached into the neck of his shirt and pulled out a key on a chain.

"You've got to be kidding." Ellie pulled the long chain over Sam's head and unlocked the door. "I hope you're not planning to wear your car keys around your neck when you get your licence."

She was glad Sam ignored her to stumble into the room. Again she reminded herself it wasn't Sam's fault. Why did Lauren's mum have to come up with such an extreme punishment?

Ellie ran her hand along the door frame as she listened to Sam run into things in the dark room. She found the switch and flicked it on. Light flooded the area and she stepped into a lounge room. To her left was a door leading into a bathroom. In the wall across from her in the right hand corner was a closed door that Sam aimed for. She guessed it must be his bedroom. On the wall to her right were another two closed doors. She locked the entrance door behind her and opened the door closest to Sam's room. It hid a set of steps. Closing it, she carefully opened the next door. It was an 'L' shaped bedroom. She walked further into the room when she realised no one was in it. The room was lit by the glow of a bedside lamp sitting on a chest of drawers next to a queen-sized bed at the far end of the room. A noise made Ellie quickly close the door and follow Sam.

He was face down on his single-sized bed, the lamp knocked off his bedside drawers. Dropping his wallet and key onto the drawers, she picked up the lamp, turning it on so she could see where it was safe to walk. One of his shoes lay near the door while he still wore the other one. A computer sat on a desk in one corner of the room, the rest of the wall taken up by a large bookcase that was haphazardly filled with books, computer games and action figures. A beanbag was at the foot of the bed and the floor had a scattering of books, computer games, crockery and clothes.

Ellie grinned when Sam started to snore. Maybe this was going to be easier than she'd thought. Hopefully the rest of the weekend would go as planned. Her gaze rested on the beanbag. Not the best option, but it was far better than the first weekend she hadn't been able to stay at Lauren's.

Ellie shuddered as she remembered spending most of that weekend at a train station. Again she pushed the memory away. Last weekend hadn't been great either. Ellie shied away from thinking of that disaster. Instead she headed back into the lounge room and crossed the room to the bathroom, locking herself in. Now for the next step in her plans. No way was she going to risk a repeat of last weekend. Her handbag was quickly opened. She pulled out her makeup bag and a bottle of baby oil, placing them on the vanity. Her dress and high heels were changed for baggy long pants, an old football jumper two sizes too big and combat boots. Her handbag looked nearly empty now. As soon as her makeup was cleaned off, Ellie used a pale foundation, black lipstick and black eyeliner. She poured baby oil into her hand and grimaced as she turned her golden blond hair into an oily, stringy mess. She grinned at the ghastly image of herself in the mirror. No one would recognise her. As soon as her gear was back in her handbag she slung it over her shoulder and opened the bathroom door.

She jumped back when she saw a young man in front of her, hand raised to open the door. She barely managed to smother the scream that threatened to break free.

Chapter Two

It took Ellie a moment to recognise Tom, Sam's older brother. At seventeen, he was little more than a year older than his brother. Some of his features were similar to Sam's and he had dark brown hair, but there the similarities ended. While Sam was called Baby Face and looked years younger, Tom could easily have passed for twenty. He had no curls like his brother and if his hair was any shorter it'd be shaved. He wore a silver stud in one ear and an identical one in his nose.

"Who the hell are you? And what are you doing in my bathroom?"

"I'm with Sam."

"Then you might as well go home. He's passed out in his room."

That was something she couldn't do. She'd thought finding someone whose parents would be away for the weekend was the solution. She hadn't taken into account a bossy older brother. Trying to remain calm, she dredged up an expression of surprise. "Already? I was only a few minutes." She tried to push past Tom.

He grabbed her by the upper arm, preventing her from moving away from him. "Who are you? Where did Sam find you? And what are you doing with my brother? He's not your type. Actually, I don't think he's anyone's type."

Ellie wrenched her arm away. "Unlike you I suppose. I bet you think you're everyone's type."

Tom smiled. "Not the answer I was looking for. I use that technique heaps. Who are you?"

"What technique?"

"Avoiding answering the main question by asking other questions or trying to sidetrack the person. Now, let's try again. Who are you?"

Ellie felt like screaming. Trust her to run into someone with a one-track mind. "Do you suffer from an obsessive compulsive disorder? I've never met anyone so focused before. It can't be natural."

"Out." Tom pointed to the outside door.

She reminded herself to remain calm. Panicking wouldn't help her deal with her latest problem. "You're getting very boring." Ellie started to walk towards the door Tom still pointed at. Before she reached it, she changed direction and headed towards Sam's room.

Tom followed, managing to step in front of her before she reached the bedroom. "What do I have to do? Call the police? You're not welcome here."

"Sam!"

Tom clamped his hand over her mouth. "Shh. Don't wake him."

Ellie stepped back and Tom dropped his hand. She glared at him. "He said I could stay the night. It's too late to organise somewhere else to stay. No one's going to appreciate me turning up on their doorstep at three in the morning."

"You could always go home."

"Not tonight I can't." She now regretted getting Sam so drunk it looked like he'd sleep through anything. Or maybe he was always a heavy sleeper. She had no idea what to do, but refused to panic. There had to be some way to convince him.

Tom sighed. "What's your name?"

She didn't think he'd recognised her, but she wasn't taking any chances. Especially since they went to the same school. "Beth." It wasn't exactly a lie. There were lots of nicknames you could use when your name was Elizabeth.

"Where were you planning to sleep?"

Ellie gestured towards the bedroom. "The beanbag." When Tom shook his head, she argued, "It's not like I haven't slept in one before. They're actually comfortable. Better than sleeping on the floor. And it's not like there's space in your brother's bed."

Tom's eyes narrowed. "How do you know we're brothers? Have we met before? When you weren't trying to look like the bride of Frankenstein?"

Ellie's mind raced as she lined up her excuse. She had to be more careful with what she said. She shrugged. "You live in the same house. He said your parents are away this weekend. Not that you look old enough to be his father. It just seemed like the most logical conclusion."

Tom yawned, his hand automatically covering his mouth. "I'm too tired for this conversation," he muttered.

"Then get out of the way and let me crash. What do you think I'm going to do? Knife you in your sleep?"

"Anything's possible."

Ellie held out her handbag. "Here. You want to check for weapons?"

Tom grinned. "Like that'd make a difference.

There's a kitchen upstairs with a block of knives that'd do the job."

"Fine! Don't let me in the bedroom." She strode to the lounge suite and dropped into the double seater. "I'll sleep here." She kicked off her boots and lay down. No pillow, no blanket. Not comfortable at all. At least she had the next weekend covered. And so far this weekend wasn't anywhere near as bad as the past two had been.

"You're persistent, I'll give you that." Tom headed for his room, disappearing inside.

Ellie stared after him. The top half of his bedroom door was visible over the back of the couch. Did that mean he'd given up trying to throw her out? She didn't know what to think. Maybe she should lock herself in Sam's room before he changed his mind. Or had he gone to call the police to kick her out? She sat up when Tom entered the room. Her gaze was drawn to the pillow and blanket in his hands. He dropped them onto her lap, heading for the bathroom without a word.

It took a few seconds for victory to register. Relief hit her. With a grin, she put the pillow at one end of the seat, shook the blanket out over herself and lay down again. When she heard the shower start, her gaze was drawn to the closed bathroom door she could see from the lounge chair. What had made him give in? She'd been certain he wasn't going to cave. And then she would've been stuck looking for somewhere else to spend the night. Her mobile phone beeped and she reached for it.

Forget me?

Ellie smiled and quickly replied with the address of where she was staying. She waited impatiently for Lauren to reply. Her phone beeped again.

Score! We're masterminds : D

Ellie grinned as she put her phone away. She wouldn't go that far. They were probably a long way from being masterminds, but it had taken a lot of asking around and planning to find someone she could con into letting her stay. She didn't have anyone else, she was close enough to, that she could ask to stay at their place. Not without them wondering what was going on. And she wasn't going to have everyone at school talking about her and wondering what the problem was. No way. She knew how harsh victims were treated. And she wasn't going to risk looking like one ever again. She ran her fingers over the small scar, on the inside of her arm. She'd bled for ages and yet the rock hadn't been that large. Pushing the image of rocks, blood and jeering kids from her mind, she rearranged the blanket again.

The bathroom door opened and Tom stepped out. Ellie's breath stopped as she stared at him. A towel was wrapped around his waist and droplets of water dotted his chest and arms. She swallowed, forcing her gaze to move away from his chest. Her gaze met his.

"You sure you don't want to take a picture?" Tom asked dryly.

"If you give me a sec I'll get my phone out."

With a shake of his head, Tom strode across the room and turned the light out. The glow from Sam's lamp fell into the room. Tom was a shadow. "Go to sleep, Beth." He strode to his room.

Ellie grinned. She'd take that as another victory for her. And she could certainly do with a few victories with the way things had been going for her lately.

* * *

Ellie opened her eyes to find Sam sitting on the floor staring at her. She quickly sat up and looked around. They were alone. She wondered how long he'd been watching her. Glancing towards the television, on the same wall as the bathroom door, she checked the time on the DVD player. Nearly midday. No wonder she was starving. Sam still watched her. If she hadn't seen him blink occasionally she would've said he was frozen.

"Morning, Sam."

"You know me?"

"Ahh, yeah. I came home with you. Remember? From the party."

Sam shook his head. "Not really." He frowned. "I was talking to Lauren. She told me I should go to the party. I don't really know her either. She told me at school. Did you look like that last night when I met you?"

"Real smooth, Sam."

Ellie turned to see Tom standing in his bedroom doorway. He wore a pair of jeans that sat low on his hips. "Morning, Tom." She frantically tried to think her way out of that mistake when she saw Tom's eyes narrow. Maybe he'd ignore it. She'd wait for him to ask how she knew his name before she worried about it.

"Can't say I'd recommend you drinking, Sam. I think it impairs your judgement in a major way." Tom continued to look at Ellie as he spoke.

"Sounds like your brother takes after you with the smooth comments." Ellie threw the blanket back and swung her feet to the floor. "I don't suppose I can get something to eat?" She turned to Sam, thinking he'd be more helpful than his brother. She wasn't wrong.

"Oh. Of course." He stumbled to his feet and hurried to the door the stairs were hidden behind.

Ellie listened to the sound of his feet against the timber tread. She heard him get about halfway up before he clambered back down. He stopped in the doorway. When he continued to stare at her silently, she bit back a sigh. "What?"

Sam blushed. "I didn't ask what you wanted for breakfast."

Tom shook his head. "What's it matter? Give her cereal. She's lucky I didn't kick her out this morning. You know what Mum'd say if she knew you had a girl stay over."

"Yeah, but–" Sam began.

"You're hopeless, Sam," Tom said.

Sam's blush deepened. He looked over to Ellie. "What would you like for breakfast?"

"What are my choices?"

"Everything."

Ellie grinned. "Everything?"

Sam nodded.

She couldn't resist. He had said everything. "Pancakes, vanilla ice cream and maple syrup."

"Okay." Sam turned and started back up the stairs.

Ellie stared after him in surprise. She looked over to Tom when he started to laugh. "What's so funny?"

"You. Your face was priceless. You honestly thought he'd say no."

"You mean he's going to make that?"

Tom nodded. "And you better eat it too."

Ellie slowly smiled. "I think I'm going to move in here permanently. That's my favourite meal." Her smile widened when Tom scowled. She rose from the lounge chair and headed for the bathroom, grabbing her bag that had slipped onto the floor.

Chapter Three

Once she'd finished in the bathroom, Ellie found the lounge room empty so she went up the stairs. She froze at the top, her feet sinking into thick carpet. The upstairs lounge room looked like it belonged in an architectural magazine. A clatter off to her right drew her attention to a kitchen. It was full of stainless steel workspaces, timber doors and was larger than both the kitchen and dining room at her house. Sam moved like he spent a lot of time in the kitchen while Tom sat on the corner of the bench that separated the kitchen from the lounge room.

When Ellie moved closer, Sam looked up. "Do you want to eat in the dining room or out on the patio?"

Ellie turned in the direction he indicated. The dining room was an octagonal area filled with tall windows and light. The patio was reached from a glass door leading out from the dining room.

Opening the door, she stepped outside and found herself looking out over a swimming pool. She walked the length of the patio and saw it was level with the ground, which dropped away like a cliff, barely a metre away. The patio only ran along part of the back of the house. She guessed it was what people called a split-level house. All she knew was that it was nothing like her house. She returned to the kitchen.

Sam flipped a pancake over in the frypan. "Did you decide?"

"Dining room?" She was feeling a little out of her element. She'd never been in a house like this before. Downstairs was nothing like upstairs. She'd never have guessed this showpiece existed. What was she doing here? Panic flared and she pushed it away. Where else could she go? What other choice did she have? None. She had to stay.

Sam flipped the pancake onto a cooling rack and poured more batter into the pan. "Tom?"

Tom slid off the bench. "You've got to be kidding. She can set the table."

"Please?" Sam took ice cream out of the freezer.

"Do you want me to help?" Ellie asked.

Tom stared at her for a moment. "You would have done better cleaning off the makeup instead of putting more on." He opened a drawer and pulled out some cutlery.

Ellie bit back the remark she wanted to make. The whole idea of the makeup was to look terrible. She shouldn't complain when she achieved her goal, but it was difficult when Tom made negative comments about the way she looked. He was heart-stopping gorgeous. Who wanted someone who looked like that thinking they were gouge-your-eyes-out ugly?

She wandered into the dining room and sat in the chair Tom pointed at. She watched as the table was transformed. A linen tablecloth, a fancy jar of maple syrup, ice cream in a cut glass serving bowl, matching cutlery, white bowls at each place and a white serving plate with hot pancakes.

It didn't take Ellie long to fill her bowl and her eyes closed as she savoured her first mouthful. She opened them to find Sam watching her again. She decided his brown eyes reminded her of puppy eyes. She glanced at Tom. His brown eyes certainly didn't bring to mind a baby animal. Ignoring the unnerving stare of Sam, she had another mouthful.

"Is it okay?" Sam still watched her.

She nodded. "Heavenly. If you keep feeding me like this I'm going to have to ask which bedroom do I get when I move in?" She grinned at the look of panic that flitted across Sam's face. Maybe it wasn't nice of her, but it was good not to be the one feeling out of their element.

"Mine."

Ellie laughed at Tom's answer. "Dream on, sweetheart."

"But I would have to insist on the makeup going and you learning what shampoo is for."

Ellie shrugged. "Then I guess I won't be moving in after all. I like my makeup and there's nothing wrong with my hair. Washing your hair too much can be damaging you know."

"Not washing it at all is taking the theory to the extreme."

Sam sat quietly, his attention on Ellie as he ate his food.

His constant stare was starting to bother her. "Where did you learn to cook like this, Sam?"

"Dad. He's a-"

Tom interrupted his brother. "He loves to cook. Made us both learn. Sam's the one with a talent for it."

"I won't argue that. These'd have to be the best pancakes I've ever tasted." Ellie scooped another spoonful into her mouth.

Sam blushed, but continued to watch Ellie. She

was glad when she'd eaten as much as possible and could escape. It was well past time to get away from Sam's unnerving gaze. It was starting to make her feel guilty again. Like she'd kicked a puppy or something. She pushed back from the table.

"If I eat another bite I'm going to explode. Do you want my bowl in the sink?" She started to rise.

Sam shook his head. "It's okay. I'll clean up."

Ellie shrugged. She wasn't going to beg him to let her help clean up. She wasn't an idiot. "Is your computer hooked up to the net?" When he nodded, she asked, "Mind if I use it for a few minutes. I want to check my emails." Sam nodded again, still staring at her, and Ellie nearly growled at him in frustration. "Any passwords on it? Or will I be able to use it without a drama?"

"No passwords. It automatically goes online when it's turned on."

She barely managed not to roll her eyes. Had she ever been this awkward? Maybe in grade one. Okay, and possibly in grade two as well. She shied away from her thoughts, preferring not to remember those years. They'd been bad enough living through once without reliving them. "Thanks."

Ellie hurried downstairs and into Sam's room. She took out her phone while she waited for the computer to start up and sent a text to Lauren. *Going online.* When she signed into her messenger, Lauren was waiting for her.

Ellie says: Missed you.

I want a kitten says: It's so not fair. One time we mess up and we're punished for life.

Ellie says: Just think if she'd caught us the night we had boys in your room : D

I want a kitten says: Okay, one time that she caught us messing up.

Ellie says: Pity she had a cold and got up to take something for it.

I want a kitten says: Yeah. Enough of my crappy life. How is yours?

Ellie says: How is my crappy life?

I want a kitten says: Ha ha, you know what I mean.

Ellie says: He made me pancakes with vanilla ice cream and maple syrup for breakfast.

I want a kitten says: When do I expect the wedding invite?

Ellie says: I know! I was amazed. My fave food of all time. And he cooks divine pancakes.

I want a kitten says: Do I take it you're having fun then?

Ellie says: No!!! He keeps staring at me all the time. It's soooo creepy.

I want a kitten says: Eww.

Ellie says: Yeah.

I want a kitten says: You want to go and do something then?

Ellie says: Can't. I need somewhere to stay tonight. Going to try and con another night out of him. If I leave, his brother'd probably put out the no vacancy sign.

I want a kitten says: Tom is hot!!!

Ellie says: He looks good in a towel too ;)

I want a kitten says: Tell me!!!

Ellie says: He turned out the light before I could take a pic : (

I want a kitten says: Seriously?

Ellie says: I was staring at him and he asked me if I wanted to take one. : D

I want a kitten says: And…

Ellie says: I don't think he took me seriously when I asked for a second to get out my phone.

I want a kitten says: Aww. I would've liked to see that picture. And I bet I'm not the only one!

Ellie says: :)

I want a kitten says: Maybe you should follow him

around with your phone waiting for the next photo op.

Ellie says: Nah. That'd be creepier than the way his brother stares at me.

I want a kitten says: : D

Ellie says: g2g. Can hear someone coming down the stairs.

I want a kitten says: Okay. Take care.

Ellie says: I will. I'll let you know where I'm crashing later. Hope it's here.

I want a kitten says: Wish it was here.

Ellie says: Me too.

I want a kitten says: Bibi.

Ellie says: Buh-bye.

Ellie signed out of her messenger and rose from the seat in time to see Sam enter his bedroom. She forced herself not to comment on the way he stared at her. The nicest comment that came to mind was, 'haven't you ever seen a female before?' She guessed alienating him wasn't the best way to convince him to let her stay another night. Besides, with his puppy dog eyes and expressive face she'd probably just end up feeling guilty again.

"So what do you normally do on a Saturday?"

Sam shrugged.

Now that was helpful. Ellie kept that thought to herself as well. "You must do something in your spare time."

Tom appeared in the doorway. "He spends most of his time on the computer or PlayStation. I'm going for a swim. Anyone interested?"

Ellie was tempted, but her makeup wasn't waterproof and she didn't have swimmers. Not to mention she'd lose the oil in her hair. She'd already lost enough on the pillowcase last night. "Nah, I might check out what PlayStation games Sam has."

Sam brightened immediately. "You play?"

Ellie headed for the door, forced to stop when Tom continued to stand in the way. She ignored Sam's question. "You could join us if you want."

Tom shook his head. "You'd be better off getting outside instead of staying in front of the TV. It's the perfect day for swimming."

"He only says that because he's the best on our school's swim team," Sam said.

"I guess that's why you've got such a well developed upper body." Ellie couldn't help smiling as she remember Tom standing in a towel. "We'll leave you to do your dumb jock thing while we be sloths in front of the TV."

Tom walked away without comment. Ellie's smile

faded. She was aware of Sam standing behind her and guessed if she turned to look at him she'd catch him staring at her again. She didn't look. She really didn't want to know for certain. "So where are these games kept?" She stepped into the lounge room.

"In the TV cabinet." Sam brushed past her and nearly ran over to the television to pull open the doors of the cabinet it sat on. Inside was a shelf of games and on the shelf above them sat a PlayStation and controllers. "Which game do you want to play?"

Ellie looked at the row of games, only the spine showing. She felt like saying, how the hell would I know? "How about you choose? Which is your favourite?"

Sam pulled out a shooter game and put it on. Her eyes glazed as he explained the basics, taking the controller he gave her. The next hour crept by as she spent most of the time dying.

"Get back, Beth. You're gonna die again." Sam sent his man in front of hers. The phone rang as Ellie died.

She gratefully dropped the controller when Sam paused the game to answer it. Standing up, she stretched. Leaving her handbag behind, she grabbed her phone and stepped outside. The path led her to the swimming pool. She watched as Tom reached the far end of the pool and pulled himself out. He dived back into the water and swam towards the shallow end. Ellie moved closer.

She grinned, choosing the camera setting on her phone. When he pulled himself out of the pool again she took a photo. She moved closer. "Smile." She took another photo when he looked up at her. Her smile faded when he strode towards her. She quickly shoved her phone in her pocket. "You were the one who told me to take a pic." She walked backwards.

"That offer expired."

Ellie turned to run inside. Tom captured her before she managed more than a few steps. She squealed as she tried to wriggle free. Turning to face him, she grabbed one of his hands as he tried to take her phone from her pocket. "Get off me. You're wet."

"Then delete that picture."

"Nope." She grinned as she managed to stop him from getting her phone again.

"I will get your phone. Give up now and hand it over."

Chapter Four

Ellie knew if it was a battle of strength she couldn't win. She met his gaze. But strength wasn't her only option. There was also distraction. Not to mention she was curious. She rose up on tiptoes so she could press her lips against his. Taking advantage of his surprise, she deepened the kiss. Within seconds she'd forgotten the reason she'd kissed him and her arms twined around his neck.

"Beth," he whispered against her lips.

The name jolted Ellie back to the present. She pulled away, gathering her scattered thoughts. "Well, you're no Frankenstein, but you weren't too bad." Turning, she quickly made her way inside. She caught the sound of his laughter as she closed the door. Seeing Sam was still on the phone, she grabbed her handbag and hurried into the bathroom.

When she saw the water damage to her makeup,

she was glad Sam's back had been to her. After she repaired her makeup, she frowned at the wet marks on her clothes, shaking her head. Her handbag wasn't bottomless. She hadn't been able to fit any more clothes into it. As much as she hated the idea, she was resigned to wearing these clothes until she could go home tomorrow. Late in the afternoon. The house would be empty then. Empty of people anyway. If past weekends were anything to go by it'd look like a disaster area.

Before she left the bathroom, Ellie sent the photos to her email address. She grinned. Now he could delete them if he wanted. She tucked the phone back into her pocket, swung the door open and stepped into the lounge room. Sam was off the phone and Tom stood in front of her, waiting.

He held out his hand as he stepped forward. Ellie was forced to retreat. She pulled her phone out and tried not to grin as she held it out to him. Tom stopped, frowning. Ellie lost the battle to keep a straight face and grinned.

"You've sent it to someone," he accused.

Ellie laughed. "You're welcome to delete it if you want." She wasn't about to let him know she'd taken two.

Tom smiled and shrugged. "Round one to you."

Ellie shook her head, still smiling. "Oh no, I think it must be round one, two and three to me." She slipped her phone back in her pocket when he didn't take it from her.

Tom became serious. "Why the makeup?"

"Why the stud in your nose?"

Tom smiled fleetingly. "You going to get out so I can have a shower or were you planning on sticking around to wash my back?"

Ellie laughed. "My phone has heaps of space still on it for photos. I bet I could make a fortune at school showing them around." When Tom said nothing, Ellie grinned. "Round four to me?"

"You go to my school?"

She had to be more careful of what she said. "If I did, I'd probably have to be insulted by the fact you don't remember me."

"With the amount of students at my school it'd be impossible to know everyone. Although if you did go to my school you mustn't wear that makeup. No one could miss seeing it."

Sam appeared at the bathroom door. "Are you coming back to play?"

"Do you play?" Ellie looked at Tom.

He shrugged. "Sometimes."

"Do you die every minute?"

"No."

"Then come and play. My dude needs another shield to hide behind."

"I can't do anything until I've had a shower. How long were you expecting me to stand here dripping?"

Ellie reached out and ran her fingers across his chest and then held them palm up. "You're nearly dry so stop whining."

Tom grabbed her wrist, taking a step forward. His lips parted to speak. He glanced at his brother then changed his mind. Letting go, he gave Ellie a gentle push in the direction of the bathroom door. "Out."

Ellie grinned when she heard the door lock behind her. Even Sam's constant stare didn't bother her for nearly an entire minute. "Ready to watch my poor dude die another million times?"

Sam nodded and headed back to the lounge suite. "Do you want me to put the game on an easier setting?"

Ellie shrugged. "I don't think it'd make that big a difference. I'm hopeless at these games. But I don't mind. At least I die spectacularly." She hesitated near the lounge chair. "Can I bring the beanbag out to sit on?"

Sam stumbled to his feet. "I'll get it for you." He

rushed away before Ellie could speak. He was back in seconds, dropping the beanbag at her feet.

"Thanks." Ellie moved it to where she wanted it, moulded the beanbag into shape and then dropped into it. She wriggled until she was comfortable. Looking over to tell Sam she was ready to play, she saw he watched her again. Now there was someone who needed to be told to take a picture. She ignored the urge to comment. He was letting her stay. And for that she could forgive him his unnerving tendency to stare. "Okay. I'm ready to die again."

Another couple of hours were taken up playing games and then Ellie hit on the idea of watching movies. They were stored in the lounge room upstairs. She looked around as she stepped onto the soft carpet. It was as perfect as it had been earlier in the day. Instead of a 'keep off the grass' sign, she felt like there should be one that read 'keep off the carpet'. She forced herself to follow Sam across the lounge room to the television cabinet he'd opened.

"I'll let you pick out some movies while I figure out what's for dinner." Sam stepped back, giving her more space.

"If it tastes even half as good as breakfast I'm sticking around to eat it."

Sam nodded, wandering over to the kitchen. Ellie

stared after him for a moment. Should she take that as a yes? She gave up trying to figure Sam out. He was odd. You couldn't figure out someone who was that odd.

She picked out five movies and closed the cabinet. A picture on the wall caught her attention. It was Tom and Sam with two older men. She looked at the next picture. The two of them were with a woman now. She guessed it was their mother. She wandered down the hallway, looking at the pictures.

"Where are you going?"

Ellie spun to face Tom. "Isn't your father around anymore?"

"What?" Tom looked puzzled.

"I haven't seen any pictures of him. Unless he was one of the really old men in that picture with you." She pointed back to the first one she'd looked at.

Sam joined them. "That's our grandfathers we were named after. Thomas and Samuel. Tom was named after our paternal grandfather, I was named after the maternal one."

"What about photos of your father? Is he camera shy?" Ellie looked from Sam to Tom.

Tom laughed. "Not at all."

Sam shook his head. "He couldn't be. He's–"

Tom interrupted his brother. "He's just never

around when photos are taken. He works long hours." He looked at the movies in Ellie's hand. "Which one are you watching first?"

She turned them so he could see the one on top. "You want to join us?"

Tom shrugged. "Might as well."

Once they were back downstairs, Ellie lay in the beanbag again, Sam in a chair across from her. Tom threw a couple of pillows, which he'd brought out of his bedroom, onto the floor. Ellie tried to concentrate on the movie, but she had two distractions. Sam kept watching her. Given time, she probably could have eventually ignored his regular glances in her direction. The second distraction was a little harder to ignore. She kept thinking back to the kiss she'd given Tom. He lay within arm's reach. Looking over at him again, her gaze was drawn to his hair. What would it feel like? Spiky? She gave into temptation and reached out to touch it, surprised his hair was softer than it looked.

Tom turned to look at her, a question on his face.

Ellie smiled slightly. "It feels different to what I thought it would."

Tom fleetingly returned her smile before he turned his attention back to the movie.

When Sam left the room to check dinner, Ellie

ran her fingers over Tom's hair again. He turned and caught her fingers in his.

"What are you playing at?" Tom sat up still holding her hand.

"It's soft. Sort of spiky, but still soft. I thought I might've been mistaken. It feels the way your brother's hair looks. What does your hair look like when you let it grow?"

"Like Sam's. I've told him he should cut his and he wouldn't look so young. It's the curls."

Ellie ran a finger along Tom's jaw line. "I don't know. His features aren't as sharp as yours. They're a lot softer. Rounded." She pulled her other hand away before he could capture it too. She tugged on the hand he held and he let her go.

"Then what's your verdict?" Tom asked.

Ellie heard footsteps on the steps and turned to see Sam enter the room. She stared at him and he stopped halfway back to his chair. He looked nervously from Ellie to his brother. Ellie rose to her feet and slowly walked over to him.

Sam licked his lips. "What's happening?"

Ellie shook her head and walked around him. When she was in front of him again, she reached up and pulled his hair tightly back. She let his hair fall around his face and turned towards Tom. "Grow it and tie it back."

"Tom?" Sam continued to stand where he'd stopped, glancing between the two of them.

"Sit down, Sam. She was just talking about how everyone should wear their hair."

"How's dinner coming along? And what are we having?" Ellie dropped into the beanbag and wriggled to get comfortable.

"Quiche. It's nearly ready."

"Good. I can smell it and it's making me hungry," Ellie said.

"Do you want a snack while you wait?" Sam was back to watching her.

Ellie shook her head. "Nah. I can wait." She frowned. "Does anyone mind if I rewind the movie? I've missed at least the last ten minutes and wouldn't have a clue what's happening." In more ways than one.

Chapter Five

Ellie stared at the time on her phone. Ten. She momentarily closed her eyes and held back the groan that wanted to escape. Dinner had been as wonderful as it had smelled. After they'd eaten, Ellie had gone online to chat to Lauren again while Tom had dressed to go out. Then she'd watched another movie with Sam. Well, she'd watched the movie while Sam had watched her. Now she leaned against the bathroom vanity and tried to talk herself into returning to the lounge room.

She sighed. She couldn't stay in here all night. Slipping her phone back into her pocket, she wished Tom was still home. But he wouldn't be back until four. At least that's what he'd said to Sam. So it would be up to her to fill in the awkward silences that regularly occurred. Ellie unlocked the door and stepped into the lounge room. Sam's gaze fell on her immediately. Ellie forced herself to yawn.

"Do you mind if I crash on your lounge chair? I don't think I got enough sleep today." Ellie gestured towards the lounge chair she'd slept on. The pillow and blanket were still there.

"Now?"

Ellie nodded. "If you don't mind." She deliberately yawned again. Anything had to be better than Sam staring at her for the rest of the night. She was beginning to feel like a specimen under a microscope. That and the awkward silences were making her extremely uncomfortable. She really had to figure out a better plan for future weekends.

"Okay." Sam turned off the television.

Ellie curled up on the lounge and watched as Sam switched off the light and retreated to his bedroom, closing the door. She tried to get comfortable. Maybe if she'd actually been tired it would've been easier to fall asleep. Trying to roll over to her other side was impossible. How had she managed to sleep here earlier that morning? She didn't know. Sitting up, she saw there was no light showing under Sam's door. She guessed he'd gone to sleep. She checked the time on her phone. Either it was broken or time was going extra slow. Only fifteen minutes had passed. She smiled. It was still at least six hours until Tom was due home. Setting the alarm on her phone to a quarter to four, she grabbed the pillow. After a glance towards Sam's door, she hurried over to Tom's room and slowly opened the door.

Once again he'd left the bedside lamp on. There wasn't anywhere near the mess Sam had in his room and drawers and wardrobes were all closed. The only real mess was the scattering of paper and books on the desk around a laptop. She strode over to the bed and dropped onto it. Sighing happily, she stretched out. Much better than the couch.

Sitting up, Ellie placed her mobile phone on the bedside drawers and turned the light off. She pushed and prodded her pillow until it was how she liked it, then lay down again. Within minutes she was asleep.

When the light came on, Ellie blinked groggily up at Tom. "Had planned to move before you came back. You must be early."

"Shove over."

"What?" Ellie yawned, trying to figure out what he meant. Sleep tugged at her and nothing made sense.

"Move over or you'll be squashed."

Ellie moved over on the bed, watching as Tom kicked off his shoes, dropped his shirt on the ground and pulled his jeans off to reveal boxers. He lay on the bed.

"Ah… Tom?" Ellie tried to focus. It always took a while for her brain to start functioning again when she was woken early.

"Go to sleep."

"The alarm on my phone will go off at a quarter to four."

Tom reached over, picked up her phone and turned off the alarm before he dropped it back on top of the drawers. Next he turned out the light and the room was plunged into darkness. Ellie considered asking him what was going on. She listened as his breathing slowed and guessed he'd gone to sleep already. Surely she'd be awake before him. Rolling over, her back to him, plenty of space between them, she returned to sleep.

* * *

Ellie slowly woke, aware of heat against her back. Her eyes blinked open and she tried to focus. She faced a wall. Frowning, she slowly turned over to find Tom lying on the bed beside her, one hand under his cheek, his eyes still closed. She smiled as she remembered the interruption to her sleep. She guessed the ghastly look she'd created had done its job. While she watched him, Tom opened his eyes.

"Morning," Ellie said softly.

Without comment, Tom rolled over and opened the top drawer. Pulling out a card of Panadol, he pushed two out and swallowed them with a mouthful of water from the bottle sitting by the lamp. Dropping the card of tablets into the drawer he left it open and fell back onto his pillow, closing his eyes. His action was almost comforting to her. She'd seen it so many times before.

She smiled. Either he'd had too much to drink last night or her makeup truly was terrible. Bad enough to give someone a headache after one glance. She looked at the alarm clock that sat behind the bottle of water. It was only seven. She still had hours to kill before she could go home.

Since one side of the bed was pushed up against the wall, her only option for getting out was to climb over Tom. When she attempted to, his eyes opened and his hands reached out to stop her. She stared down at him, trying to hold her body off his, when all she wanted to do was relax against him. But she didn't want to give him the wrong idea. That would've made all the effort of applying the makeup a waste of time.

"Where are you going?"

"To get a kitchen knife. Any preference?"

"A sharp one. The steel is in the second drawer."

Ellie grinned. "Bathroom."

Tom smiled slightly and let her go. She was nearly at the bedroom door when he called out. "Beth."

She took a few steps back so she could see past the corner of the 'L' shaped room. "What?"

He held up her phone.

She walked back to the bed and tried to take it. He held tight. "Now what?"

"When are you leaving?"

"Today."

"You don't know Sam. You've got nothing in common with him. Surely there was somewhere else you could've stayed last night."

Ellie shrugged. "I was already here."

"Why do I think there's more to the story than that?"

Ellie met Tom's gaze. She didn't need this. It was the exact thing she'd been worried might happen. Next time her and Lauren looked for someone for her to stay with she was going to insist they find an only child. "You've been watching too much TV. What do you think I am? Some criminal mastermind?"

"I'll figure it out." Tom grinned, letting go of the phone. "I'm persistent."

"Obsessive." Ellie turned and walked away. Obviously this wasn't somewhere she could stay in the future. She had a year and a bit left of school. There was no way she was going to end up being picked on again. Her fingers involuntarily rubbed against the scar on her arm. Opening the door, she stopped abruptly when she saw Sam sitting in the lounge room watching Tom's door. Looking away from him, she headed straight for the bathroom. She couldn't get a break today. Which wasn't good since the day had barely begun.

When she was finished, she stood in front of the bathroom door and stared at it. Her stomach rumbled. She guessed she had to leave the sanctuary of the bathroom soon, but she needed to come up with a plan first. She kept drawing a blank. She couldn't think of a single plausible excuse for why she'd stayed here last night. The first night was easily explained. It had been too late to go anywhere else. And Tom knew perfectly well she wasn't interested in Sam. She didn't know what Sam thought. And she didn't want to know what he thought. Some days she was barely able to figure out what she thought without worrying about anyone else.

Taking a deep breath, she slowly let it out. There was no point stalling. Squaring her shoulders, she stepped out of the bathroom. Sam had moved so he could watch the bathroom door. Creepy. She managed to suppress the urge to tell him to quit staring at her, but only just. Her mess wasn't Sam's fault. It was no point taking it out on him. Especially since he'd been nice to her in his own fashion.

"Ahh… I was wondering about breakfast."

Sam jumped to his feet. "What would you like?"

"The same as yesterday?"

Sam nodded enthusiastically, dashing from the room. Ellie sighed. She'd been going to ask him if she could use his computer. She eyed the stairwell. She wasn't about to seek him out. He hadn't minded yesterday, so she guessed it'd be okay today.

In Sam's room she found his computer was already on. She quickly signed into her messenger and saw Lauren wasn't online. Lauren was usually an early riser, but on the rare occasion, she slept in. She considered sending her a text to wake her, but decided that was mean. Instead she left a message.

Ellie says: All's well. My stalker is making me breakfast.

Ellie says: Tom doesn't snore ;)

Grinning, she signed out. She bet Lauren would text her the moment she woke up. She was right. Midmorning the text came through. *Details!!! I'm online.*

Chapter Six

Ellie was relieved to have an excuse to take a break from the game she played with Sam. She was being slaughtered. Sam hadn't lost a single life and she was beginning to feel annoyed she still played as terrible as yesterday. The game didn't look that difficult, so why was she still dying all the time?

"Can I use your computer again?"

Sam nodded.

"You can play without me for a while. It's not going to make any difference to the game for you if I'm not helping. Actually, it probably will make a difference. You might win for a change." She grinned.

Sam only nodded.

Ellie's grin faded. "Ah… okay then." She entered his room and signed into her messenger. Several of her friends were online so she quickly set her status as busy.

Want kitten now says: Tell me everything.

Ellie says: About?

Want kitten now says: Details now or you die slowly.

Ellie says: There's nothing to tell.

Want kitten now says: Then why the snoring comment?

Ellie says: You weren't online. I was just hassling you.

Want kitten now says: : P

Ellie says: : D

Want kitten now says: So nothing interesting happened?

Ellie says: I took over Tom's bed while he was out. Had planned to be out of it before he got home. But, he returned early.

Want kitten now says: And? The suspense is killing me. He wasn't like the octopus from hell, was he?

Ellie says: No. He crashed and that was all. And please don't remind me of last weekend. I still find it hard to believe Brody acted like that.

Want kitten now says: But nothing happened with Tom?

Ellie says: Nothing. I don't think either of them are like Brody. I think I might have been worried about nothing.

Want kitten now says: You slept in Tom's bed with him?

Ellie says: Yep : D

Want kitten now says: I know girls at school who'd pay for him just to look at them. You have all the luck. What's he like? Is he a bed hog?

Ellie says: Nah. He stayed on his side.

Want kitten now says: : (

Ellie says: lol. That's exactly the way I wanted it. So quit with the sad face.

Want kitten now says: What sort of bed does he have?

Ellie says: *rolls eyes* queen-size.

Want kitten now says: Nice. What sort of sheets?

Ellie says: Lauren!

Want kitten now says: Nothing interesting ever happens to me. You've got to tell me everything.

Ellie says: At school tomorrow.

Want kitten now says: Come early.

Ellie says: NO!

Want kitten now says: You're no fun.

Ellie says: You'll live.

Want kitten now says: No I won't. I'll have died of curiosity by then.

Ellie says: Bad luck.

Want kitten now says: Harsh.

Ellie says: Yep.

Want kitten now says: What are you doing today?

Ellie says: Don't know? You?

Want kitten now says: Grounded : (Have to clean my room before I can do anything. It's going to take me a week to get it cleaned up.

Ellie says: Wish I could help you.

Want kitten now says: Me too. You're so much quicker than me.

Ellie says: Probably all the cleaning experience I've gained in the past three years. Better go. Sam's waiting for me.

Want kitten now says: Your stalker?

Ellie says: : D

Want kitten now says: He still doing the creepy stare?

Ellie says: Yep.

Want kitten now says: Eww.

Ellie says: Yep.

Want kitten now says: K. Bibi.

Ellie says: Buh-bye.

Ellie continued to stare at the screen after she'd signed out. If the teenage years were meant to be some of the best years of your life, like her teachers kept telling her, she dreaded to think what her future held. Sighing heavily, she returned to the lounge room. Tom came out of his room at the same moment. Their gazes met and held for a moment before Tom looked away and headed for the bathroom. Turning back towards the television, she found Sam staring at her. She fought the urge to run screaming from the room. She only had to survive until the afternoon. Then she could go home. There should be a bus stop somewhere around here. Hopefully she had enough money for a bus home. After lunch she'd look online to see where the closest one was.

* * *

Sam walked with her to the timber gate. He gave her a piece of paper. She glanced down at it and saw it was a phone number. She looked back at Sam who continued to stare at her.

He blushed. "Our phone number."

No kidding! She managed to stop the comment from escaping. He might have spent the weekend staring at her unnervingly, but at least he'd let her stay without questioning why she'd wanted to. "Thanks." She shoved the number in her pocket, glancing up when the gate swung open. It was Tom. She'd hoped to be gone before he returned.

"What? No plans to have your mail redirected here?" Tom stepped out of the way.

"Try to contain your disappointment."

Tom laughed. "I'll be heart broken."

"Take two Panadol and you'll be pain free in minutes." Ellie turned to Sam when he made a strange squeaking sound.

Tom swore. "Looks like Mum's home early." He turned to Sam. "Disappear."

Sam didn't need any extra encouragement. He ran down the steps and in the door at the foot of them. Ellie looked at Tom in confusion. Beside them the garage door opened automatically and a car drove in.

"What's going on?" Ellie asked.

"The least you can do is play along." He dropped an arm around her shoulders.

"What are my lines?"

"As little as possible." Tom guided her forward.

A woman, with curly brown hair tied back from her face and a fringe of ringlets, came out of the garage. She looked like she was dressed for a business meeting with her slim black skirt and black jacket over an ice blue blouse. "Tom?"

"Just breezing through. Left my phone at home." Tom continued to stand with his arm around Ellie.

"Are you going to introduce us?" The woman looked pointedly at Ellie.

"Mum, this is Beth. I'll be back after I give her a lift home. Beth, my mum, Teresa."

Ellie held out her hand. "Pleased to meet you. I was just admiring your front yard. Someone must spend a lot of time taking care of it."

Teresa hesitated before she took Ellie's hand. "Yes. The gardener."

Ellie ignored the frosty tone and smiled. "Well he's certainly worth what you're paying him. It looks great."

Tom's hand tightened on her shoulder. "I'll be back for dinner."

"I hope you don't mind we're not sticking around. I'm desperate to get home and clean this makeup off and wash my hair. Tom picked me up from the play I've been acting in." Ellie grinned. "The things we do for extracurricular activities."

Teresa thawed slightly. "Maybe next time you'll be able to stay a little longer."

Tom led Ellie to his car that was parked on the

footpath. He held the passenger door open for her. The look he gave her when he closed the door made her wonder why he was so annoyed.

Ellie waited until he started the car. "What's your problem?"

"What part of saying as little as possible didn't you understand?"

"The middle?" Ellie grinned when Tom remained silent. She spotted a bus stop. "Can you drop me there?"

"Not likely. Where do you live?"

"You've got to be kidding."

"Not at all. You know where we live. So what's the problem?"

Ellie sighed. She gave him the name of the closest shopping centre to her place instead. Tom remained silent as he continued to drive. Several glances towards him showed he still looked annoyed. When he pulled up in front of the shopping centre, about twenty minutes later, he was still silent.

"Thanks for the lift." Ellie unbuckled, turning to open the car door. Tom's hand landing on her shoulder caused her to face him again. "What?"

"Are you in some sort of trouble?"

"No."

"Your parents weren't bothered you were away the entire weekend?"

Ellie grinned. "Nice try."

Tom shook his head. "Come on, Beth. How old are you? Fifteen? Sixteen? Not many parents let their kids disappear for the weekend."

"Sixteen. I live with my mum. Dad's a few hours from here."

"I bet that hurt."

Ellie frowned. "What?"

"Giving me some info about yourself."

Ellie laughed. "Traumatic." She started to turn her head. Tom's hand, that still rested on her shoulder, slid behind her head and pulled her forward. Their lips met and it was her turn to be surprised. Her hands automatically entwined at his neck as she leaned closer.

"Where do you live?" Tom murmured against her lips.

Ellie pulled back far enough to meet his gaze. She smiled slightly. "Keep trying. Better luck next time." She grinned, starting to pull away.

Tom captured her arm, pulling up her sleeve. He took a pen from the centre console and wrote a mobile number on her skin. "Text me. Let me know you got home okay."

"I can take care of myself. I don't need a babysitter."

"Humour me."

Ellie sighed. "Fine." Tom released her and she climbed out of the car. The electric window slid down as she closed the door. She leaned on the sill, looking back in at him. "What?"

"Say hi to Frank for me."

Remembering his bride of Frankenstein comment, Ellie grinned and stepped away from the car. She waved as he drove off. Still smiling, she headed for home. It was only a ten minute walk. As she entered her street, her smile faded. It was nothing like the neighbourhood Tom and Sam lived in. The only gardeners in her area would be the ones paid to take care of other people's yards. They certainly didn't take care of their own. She walked through the gate that hung crooked on its hinges. Grass grew up through the rusty mesh. The concrete path that led to her front door was cracked and prickles had taken up residence in them. Ellie took larger steps to avoid standing on them.

When she reached the verandah, which ran across the front of the small timber house, she pulled her key from her pocket. Avoiding the loose floorboard, she unlocked the door and stepped into the open plan lounge, kitchen and dining area. Letting the door slam shut behind her, she dropped her handbag in a clear spot near the door, her eyes narrowing at the mess.

Chapter Seven

The sofa had a stain in the middle where something had been spilt. Empty spirit and beer cans littered the area and a plastic bowl of chips had been knocked over and trod into crumbs. Luckily lino was easy to clean. Ignoring the dirty dishes that filled the sink and littered the kitchen and island benches, Ellie pulled a large garbage bag from the bottom kitchen drawer. While she was in the middle of throwing empty containers into the black plastic bag, her mum stumbled out of her bedroom, a ratty dressing gown hanging open to show her short, silky nightie.

Sharon yawned, finger combing her shoulder length sandy blond hair. "You look like crap."

Ellie eyed her mum. "You don't look much better." She grabbed a card of Panadol off the top of the fridge and threw them towards her mum.

Sharon popped two out, hesitated and popped out a

third. Swallowing them dry, she tossed the card onto the island bench. "Your father rang. Something about next weekend. Told him you'd be home tonight if he wanted to talk to you." She shrugged and headed for the bathroom.

Ellie picked up the card of tablets and returned them to the top of the fridge. Noticing it was the last card left, she made a mental note to pick up more when she went shopping.

While Ellie was outside dropping the two bags of garbage into the wheelie bin, she pulled out her phone and sent a text to Tom. *Home safe and sound Ma.* She smiled as she returned it to her pocket. She'd waited to send the text so he didn't know how close she lived to the shopping centre. She was in the middle of washing dishes when her phone beeped. Drying her hands on her pants, she checked the message. *Wrong gender. Are you sure you go to school?* Ellie laughed before she returned to the dishes.

A little over an hour later, she surveyed the living area. A towel covered the stain on the sofa and would hopefully soak up what had smelled like scotch and coke, the floors were still damp from being mopped and every window was open to clear out the smell of stale alcohol and smoke. The bathroom had been cleaned, she shuddered as she recalled the mess in there, and she'd eaten a sandwich for dinner. She'd been surprised to find four pieces of bread still in the fridge. She wistfully wondered what Tom and Sam were having for dinner.

Ellie shrugged. There was no point in stressing about it. Until recently, living with her mum had been the best choice. She still thought it was better than moving in with her father. As long as she kept the house clean, stayed away on weekends and didn't bring home trouble, her mum didn't care what she did. She could pretty much live her own life. It was just a pain that her years of staying with Lauren on the weekend were over. But she was sure she could figure something out. Eventually. She didn't have a choice. There was no way she could live with her father full time.

Snatching up her bag from near the front door, Ellie stopped at her bedroom door, which was just past the bathroom. She used the other key on her key ring to unlock the padlock on the barrel bolt she'd attached to her door, swinging it shut behind her as she turned on the light.

She'd learned the hard way that when people were drunk they'd enter any room that wasn't locked and make themselves at home. Once she dropped her bag on her bed, she turned to pull clothes from her duchess. She desperately needed a shower. Her hair was driving her crazy, her makeup felt five centimetres thick and she was sick of wearing the same clothes.

After a shower, Ellie sat at her laptop and turned it on. She towel dried her hair while she waited. It was a few minutes after eight. Less than an hour and Lauren would have to go to bed. Leaving her towel draped around her shoulders, she signed into her messenger.

Kitten, kitten, kitten says: You were ages.

Ellie says: Had to clean up the mess.

Kitten, kitten, kitten says: Was it bad?

Ellie says: At least no one threw up on the floor this weekend.

Kitten, kitten, kitten says: Eww.

Ellie says: I know!

Kitten, kitten, kitten says: You sure it's worth it?

Ellie says: Alternative- Dad, Pamela, clone 1, clone 2.

Kitten, kitten, kitten says: Okay, you're right.

Ellie says: Exactly. I'd rather clean up vomit every day of the week than listen to Pamela saying, isn't there something else you should be doing? I'm sure I didn't spend my childhood sprawled in front of a tv/listening to music/on the computer. Must you sit like that? What are you wearing? And my favourite one of all, must you always try to be such a disappointment to your father?

Kitten, kitten, kitten says: I hope I never have to meet her.

Ellie says: Did I tell you I organised to stay there next weekend?

Kitten, kitten, kitten says: Yep. You're crazy.

Ellie says: Probably. But until I can figure out something else, they'll have to do. I couldn't live there full time. I don't think Pamela would let me anyway.

Kitten, kitten, kitten says: I bet she was behind your dad's offer of sending you to boarding school last year.

Ellie says: More than likely.

Ellie says: I've just had someone try to add me as a contact. Give me a minute while I add them and see who it is.

Kitten, kitten, kitten says: I have to go anyway. Mum keeps hassling me to get my room finished. Think you can sneak in tomorrow after school and help me? They're going to be gone until at least six. Dad has to work late and Mum said she's grabbing some groceries after work.

Ellie says: K. No problem.

Kitten, kitten, kitten says: You're the best.

Ellie says: I know : P

Kitten, kitten, kitten says: Bibi.

Ellie says: Buh–bye.

Still smiling after her conversation with Lauren, Ellie sent a message to the person who wanted to add her to their contacts.

Ellie says: Who's this?

Society of Australian Magicians says: Sam Wallace. You signed into your messenger on my computer.

Ellie says: Hi Sam. Tom didn't get in trouble for me being there, did he?

Society of Australian Magicians says: No.

Ellie says: That's good.

Society of Australian Magicians says: Is that why you came home with me?

Ellie says: ???

Society of Australian Magicians says: To be with Tom.

Ellie says: No.

Society of Australian Magicians says: Why did you come home with me?

Ellie says: Why are you only asking me now? You could have asked me while I was there.

Ellie says: You still there?

Society of Australian Magicians says: Yeah.

Society of Australian Magicians says: Tom wants to ask you something.

TW has been added to the conversation.

TW says: Ma?

Ellie says: : D

Ellie says: Is that going to bother you for life?

TW says: Makes me wonder if you do go to school. Do you?

Ellie says: Yep.

TW says: Not homeschooled?

Ellie says: Nope.

TW says: Which school?

Ellie says: Sam- is he always so stubborn?

Society of Australian Magicians says: Yeah.

Ellie says: It's almost like a disorder.

TW says: Funny.

Society of Australian Magicians says: They said he was untreatable : D

Ellie says: That wouldn't surprise me.

TW says: You're a pair of comedians.

Ellie says: Yep.

TW says: I still want to know why you stayed this weekend.

Society of Australian Magicians says: I already asked her.

Ellie says: Maybe it's a disorder that runs in the family. Do your parents have trouble dropping a subject?

TW says: I will figure it out eventually.

Society of Australian Magicians says: He always does.

Ellie says: What did you have for dinner tonight?

TW says: What?

Ellie says: The last meal of the day… dinner. You have heard of it, haven't you?

TW says: You're hilarious.

Ellie says: : D

Ellie says: Well, what was it?

Society of Australian Magicians says: Marinated chicken legs on a bed of rice with stir-fry veges.

Ellie says: Who cooked it?

Society of Australian Magicians says: Dad.

Ellie says: What's he cook like?

Society of Australian Magicians says: Better than me.

Ellie says: Wish I could have stayed for dinner. : (

TW says: You almost moved in.

Ellie says: Nah, I didn't bring a suitcase

TW says: So we lock the door if you turn up with a suitcase?

Society of Australian Magicians says: You're

welcome to come have dinner Wednesday night if you want.

TW says: Only if you don't wear that makeup and dress like a bag lady.

Society of Australian Magicians says: I'm cooking Wednesday. Dad works late that night.

Ellie says: Sounds interesting, but I don't know if I can make it.

TW says: Did you suddenly become busy before or after I said no makeup?

Society of Australian Magicians says: I don't mind.

TW says: Mum will.

Society of Australian Magicians says: We can have it in our lounge room. Then she wouldn't know.

TW says: Dining room or our lounge room- no makeup.

Ellie says: Sure thing, Ma.

Society of Australian Magicians says: Is that a yes? You coming to dinner?

Ellie says: I don't know. I'll have to get back to you.

Society of Australian Magicians says: kk

Society of Australian Magicians says: g2g. Bedtime. 9pm.

Ellie says: K. Night.

Society of Australian Magicians has left the conversation.

Ellie says: What about you? Need to go to bed?

TW says: Nah. I go when I'm tired.

Ellie says: That seems odd. Why has Sam got a bedtime then?

TW says: He won't when he turns seventeen.

Ellie says: K.

TW says: You?

Ellie says: Me what?

TW says: Have a bedtime.

Ellie says: Nah. When I'm tired.

Ellie says: Been like that since I was thirteen.

TW says: Unusual.

Ellie says: *shrugs* If you think so.

TW says: Why since you were thirteen?

Ellie says: My father moved out. Mum's more laid back.

TW says: Laid back or couldn't care less?

Ellie says: Laid back.

TW says: Hmm.

Ellie says: What's that mean?

TW says: That I'm slowly putting the pieces of the puzzle together.

Ellie says: You haven't got any pieces to put together.

TW says: More than you think.

Ellie says: Like what.

TW says: : D

Ellie says: Oh don't be a bastard.

TW says: I might head to bed. I have swimming practice in the morning.

Ellie says: Is that every morning?

TW says: Weekdays only.

Ellie says: How early do you have to get up?

TW says: Five.

Ellie says: Rather you than me.

TW says: I don't mind. And I love swimming.

Ellie says: Why?

TW says: Always have.

Ellie says: That's not an answer.

TW says: Why is pancakes, vanilla ice cream and maple syrup your favourite food?

Ellie says: You've made your point.

TW says: Where do you live?

Ellie says: Thought you were going to bed.

TW says: Night. : D

Ellie says: Night.

Chapter Eight

Still smiling, Ellie closed down her laptop, leaving her towel draped over the back of her chair as she rose to her feet. Hearing the television on, she wandered out to the lounge room. Sharon was sprawled on the sofa, a coffee cup in one hand and a sandwich in the other.

"Night, Mum."

Sharon looked up. "Did you have a good weekend?"

"Yeah, it was all right. You?"

"Reasonable. Did your father ring you back?"

Ellie shook her head. "Nah. Guess it wasn't important."

"Probably that stupid bitch he married wanting to make sure you bring the right sort of clothes. I don't know what she's on. You're old enough to pick out your own clothes. I wonder if she's going to keep dressing her clones like her when they're teenagers."

Ellie laughed. Her stepsisters did look like clones of their mother, right down to the clothes she dressed them in. At the ages of eight and six it was starting to lose its cute factor. Not that it had ever had much of one. "Can you imagine them in ten years? All dressed the same. Wonder if that means Pamela will dress too young for her age or they'll have to dress too old for their ages."

Sharon snorted. "As if Stupid Bitch would wear something that was inappropriate. They'll have to dress too old for their age."

They fell silent for a moment, grinning at each other. Ellie broke the silence. "I need to get some groceries tomorrow afternoon. We're cleaned out."

"I'll leave my keycard on the bench when I head to work."

The familiarity of the conversation made her feel a little more in control of her life. Now if she could just get her weekends sorted out again. "Thanks. I'll see you tomorrow night."

Sharon nodded and turned back to the television.

* * *

Ellie grabbed at her textbooks as they started to slip from her arms. She couldn't believe she'd slept through her alarm clock and ended up arriving late to school. Looking down to position the books better, she hurried around the corner of the corridor. The books skidded across the floor when she collided with someone. Looking up when they grabbed her upper arms to steady her, she met Tom's gaze.

Tom grinned. "Did you ditch Frankie?"

Ellie suppressed a groan. It looked like she'd have been better off continuing to sleep rather than rush to get to class on time. "Frankie?" She shook her head thoughtfully. "No. I don't know a Frankie."

"Give it up, Beth." Tom stressed her name.

Lauren came running around the corner, waving a textbook. "Ellie you forgot… oh." She came to a sudden halt when she saw Tom.

"Ellie?" Tom stepped back from her, his lips thinning.

Ellie stared at him defiantly. "Elizabeth."

Lauren came forward, pushed the book at Ellie and fled back the way she'd come.

"And that explains the name you use online." Tom bent to pick up the books.

Ellie joined him. "You should be happy you figured out who I am. What was it?"

"Your eyes." He handed the books to her as they stood up.

"I should have used coloured contacts."

"Demon eyes?"

"I was thinking skull and crossbones would have looked good."

Tom reluctantly smiled. "Why did you stay the weekend?"

Ellie rolled her eyes. "Get over it already. You're annoying the hell out of me."

"I guess if I ask around I'll figure it out eventually."

Ellie took a deep breath, trying not to let the panic show on her face. That was the last thing she wanted. "Fine. But not now. I don't have time for this discussion. After school."

"What's wrong with lunchtime?"

"I have other plans." Like getting Lauren to help her come up with an excuse.

"You disappear and I will ask around."

"All right. You said that already." Ellie stepped past him without another word. She was going to be extremely late for her first class. She sighed. Great start to the day. Not!

By the time the bell rang for lunch, Ellie was desperate to talk to Lauren. She didn't have a clue what she could tell Tom. Her home life might be a little different, but it was no one's business except hers. It looked like she was going to have to go to her father's place every weekend. She hated to even think about it and wasn't sure which was worse. Spending the night at the train station or putting up with Pamela. Staying at Brody's house certainly wasn't an option. Once had been one time too many and neither her nor Lauren had spoken to him since. Even when he'd tried to apologise.

Ellie reached the tree her and Lauren always sat under and dropped to the ground. Her stomach grumbled and she ignored it. Until she went shopping that afternoon there was no food in the house. Her mum's party friends always cleaned the fridge and cupboards out. She normally stashed some food in her room, but she'd been too worried about where she was going to stay to remember. Finding bread in the fridge last night had almost been a miracle.

Lauren dropped down beside Ellie. "You have to tell me everything about your weekend." She bit into her sandwich.

"Seriously, it wasn't that interesting." She tried not to stare at Lauren's food.

Lauren shook her head. "You're not getting out of it that easily. What did Sam say when he found out he went home with Cinderella and woke up with the ugly stepsister?"

Ellie laughed. "I'm not sure he remembered. You had already got a few drinks into him before I continued. He didn't remember me at all. But Tom kept hassling me about why I was there. Seriously, it wasn't as easy as I'd thought it'd be."

"Why's that?"

"Tom's determined to find out why I stayed the weekend. Help me think up a good excuse." Ellie tried to ignore the sandwich Lauren was eating. She knew Lauren would willingly hand it over, but it wouldn't be fair to let her friend go hungry. There hadn't even been anything in the house for breakfast.

"How about it was an elaborate set up so you could attend the party without parental permission, but part of the planning fell through and you had nowhere to stay for the weekend because your best friend was grounded."

Ellie looked thoughtful. "Pretty good. Better not say best friend since you were at the party too."

Lauren grinned. "Good point."

"I don't think I'll be able to help you clean your room this arve. He's expecting me to meet him after school and explain everything."

"Aww, Ellie! Come on. I'm desperate."

"So am I."

Lauren sighed. "Okay. How about Tuesday? We'll only have until five though."

"Yeah. Tuesday's free."

"Great! Now tell me every detail. Even the boring stuff."

Ellie grinned and the rest of the lunch hour was spent discussing the weekend in depth. When the bell rang, Ellie reluctantly dragged herself to her next class. She knew the rest of the day would crawl by. She couldn't believe she'd forgotten to stash some food. In each classroom she kept watch on the hands of the clock, her stomach feeling hollow. A few minutes before the last bell rang, she felt her phone vibrate in her pocket as a text came through. While the teacher was busy, she pulled it out and held it under the desk. She glanced down. It was from Tom. He'd sent directions of where to meet. Frowning, she returned the phone to her pocket, hoping he didn't want to grill her too long. She was desperate to get something to eat.

Tom was leaning against the bonnet of his car when she reached him. She frowned when she saw a couple of his friends standing nearby. He better not expect her to tell him in front of them. Although the story she'd come up with wasn't too bad. Unless of course you knew how laid back Sharon was. Ellie began to worry. What if he'd asked around about her and learned her mum let her do pretty much anything. It was too late now. She didn't have another story to tell him. As she reached the car, she saw Sam in the backseat.

Tom pushed away from the car. "Well, hop in the front. I don't have all day." He turned to his friends. "See ya tomorrow." He slid into the driver's seat and started the engine.

Ellie hurried around and hopped in. She barely had time to buckle up before he was reversing out of the car park. She turned towards the back of the car. "Hi, Sam."

Sam nodded solemnly.

Ellie sat forward again. "Think you could drop me at the same shopping centre?"

"What's wrong with letting me drop you at home?"

"I've got to get some groceries. The place is Mother Hubbard bare." Her stomach grumbled as if to underline the statement.

Tom looked sceptical. "There's nothing at all in your fridge?"

"Butter, half a jar of jam and a six-pack. I don't think school would've been happy if I'd brought beer for lunch." She turned when Sam tapped her on the shoulder. She looked at the clear plastic container he held out, her gaze drawn to the slice of cake inside. Maybe he used the right name on his messenger after all. He was a magician. "Thanks." Taking the container, she opened it, biting into the cake. Apple and cinnamon exploded in her mouth. "Mmm, heavenly. Who made this?"

"I did," Sam said softly.

"You're a magician in the kitchen." Ellie reluctantly popped the last piece of cake in her mouth, handing the container back to him.

Sam shoved the container in his schoolbag. "Are you coming for dinner Wednesday night?"

"Ahh…"

"What's the issue now?" Tom demanded. "We know who you are and before the day ends I'll know where you live. Whether or not you give me your address."

"How?"

Tom smiled cryptically. "You have secrets…"

"You look beautiful without that other makeup," Sam said.

Ellie looked back to see him watching her again. "Ahh… thanks."

"So why did you crash at our place on the weekend?"

Ellie faced forward so she could answer Tom's question. She took a deep breath and told the story her and Lauren had cooked up. She waited for Tom's comment. Instead he said nothing. He turned into the car park of the shopping centre and found an empty spot. When he opened his door, Ellie blurted out, "What are you doing?"

Tom smiled. "Going shopping with you, then dropping you home."

Ellie opened her mouth to argue. She met his determined stare. "Fine! You can push the trolley." She left her schoolbag in the car and only took her handbag. It was about a quarter of the size of the one she'd used on the weekend. Heading for the supermarket, she stopped near the trolleys and looked pointedly at Tom.

Chapter Nine

Tom grinned as he pulled a trolley out of the bay and followed her into the supermarket. Sam trailed quietly behind his brother throughout most of the expedition. He didn't remain quiet when they reached the frozen department and Ellie placed a selection of pre-cooked meals in the trolley.

"They aren't very healthy."

"I don't cook. Besides, I put fruit in there." Ellie pointed to the five apples.

When Sam opened his mouth to speak again, Tom interrupted him. "Forget it, Sam. It's her health. Or lack of."

"Not everyone has someone to teach them to cook. And the Home Ec teacher strongly advised me not to take the subject again after I managed to cause seven fires in grade eight." Ellie glared at Tom.

Tom looked at her in disbelief before he burst out laughing. "Seven?"

"Yes. I refuse to take credit for the eighth one. I wasn't at fault that time."

"Seven?"

Ellie's hands went to her hips as she continued to glare at Tom. "What are you? Deaf?"

"I'll teach you," Sam said.

"Maybe you better teach her at her house. Mum and Dad wouldn't be too happy if she burned the house down," Tom said.

Ellie ignored Tom and turned to Sam. She shrugged. "I don't know. It doesn't seem much point. I'd only be cooking for myself."

"Don't you live with your mum?" Sam asked.

Ellie nodded. "Yeah, but she works long hours during the week. I barely get to see her let alone eat a meal with her."

"Oh." Sam fell silent again.

Ellie headed for the checkout and waited in line. She was glad it didn't take long. The packet of chips she'd thrown into the trolley was starting to look really good. She opened them up as soon as she'd paid for the groceries with her mum's keycard and they were headed back to the car.

"Who'd you steal the card from? Or isn't your

name Elizabeth? Are you really Sharon Malloy?" Tom loaded the bags of groceries into the boot of his car.

"It's my mum's. She doesn't have time to go shopping. She works twelve hours a day Monday to Thursday and half a day on Friday. By the weekend she's ready to relax, not go shopping."

Tom hopped in the car and started it as soon as everyone was in. "So where do you live?"

Ellie hesitated before she told him. At least getting a lift home with the groceries would be a lot easier than buying them two shopping bags at a time and walking back and forth to the shop until it was done. Her mum might not notice the odd twenty or thirty dollars cash withdrawn when she payed for groceries but she complained if too much money was taken out. That meant a taxi was out of the question if she wanted to have any money to spend on herself.

"Anyone'd think it was a national secret." Tom glanced over his shoulder before he reversed out of the car park.

"I just don't want people thinking they can drop in whenever they feel like it." Especially not on a weekend. "Turn right."

"Why would we drop in unannounced?"

Ellie shrugged. "People do." They fell silent except for the handful of directions Ellie gave. She watched

Tom carefully when he pulled up in front of her house. His expression remained neutral and he said nothing.

Between the three of them they carried all the groceries inside. Ellie quickly put everything away while Tom and Sam prowled around the small house. Ellie closed the fridge, turned to move away and nearly stumbled over Tom.

"I thought you said there was a six-pack in there. I only saw two beers." Tom gestured towards the fridge.

Ellie wasn't about to say her mum had probably had them for breakfast. She shrugged. "So I exaggerated. Two beers, six pack," she shrugged again. "What's it matter? The fridge was still empty."

Sam joined them by the fridge. "Why's there a barrel bolt and a padlock on one of the doors?"

"I like my privacy."

Sam's mouth dropped open. After a few seconds pause he shook his head. "That's your bedroom?"

"What do you keep in there? The dead bodies of your ex-boyfriends?" Tom went to check the door for himself.

"It's to keep Frankenstein from running away," Ellie said dryly.

"Frankenstein is actually the name of the man who

created the monster. He never named his monster," Sam said.

"Ah… okay." Ellie followed Tom.

Tom lifted the padlock and let it drop back against the door. "Are you going to open it?"

"Why?"

"So I'm not left wondering what's in there and asking around if anyone's been in the sacred room that's always bolted shut." When Ellie remained silent, Tom said, "Well?"

She glared at him. He knew. She shouldn't have given in so quickly earlier. Pulling out her key, she unlocked the room. She'd spent the first few years of primary school being thought odd and getting picked on. She knew what it was like to be bullied and even had the scar to prove it. When she'd changed schools, she'd made sure she fit in. Maybe she didn't completely follow the crowd and maybe she only had one real friend. She wasn't spending her hours away from school being someone she wasn't, but she also didn't have a reputation for being odd. And she wasn't about to gain such a reputation ever again. She swung the door open and entered her room, hooking the padlock onto the barrel bolt on the other side of the door.

Tom stepped into the room. "It looks fairly ordinary to me."

"I just don't like my mum snooping in my stuff." Ellie held the drawer of her duchess closed when Tom tried to open it. "I don't like anyone snooping in my stuff." The doorway behind Tom was empty and Ellie wondered where Sam was.

Tom glanced behind him, swinging the bedroom door shut. "Why don't I believe your little story you told in the car about sneaking out to the party?"

"I didn't sneak out. I tried to arrange things so I didn't have to." She took a step away from Tom.

Tom moved closer. "Nothing adds up about you. If your mum works as many hours as you say, why don't you live in a more expensive house?"

"She prefers to invest her money elsewhere." Like alcohol. That thought she was definitely keeping to herself.

"Why did you really stay at our place?"

"I already told-"

"I don't think you've spoken a single word of truth since I've met you, Ellie." Tom stressed her name.

Ellie suddenly grinned. "Now that's where you're wrong. Every time I do tell you the truth you don't believe me."

"Name one instance."

She laughed softly. "When I told you to give me a second to get my phone out so I could take a photo."

Tom took another step forward. "Be serious."

There was only centimetres between them. Her gaze dropped to his lips. It was tempting, but they were alone in her bedroom and she wasn't going to risk him thinking it was an invitation for more than she was willing to offer.

"Well?"

Ellie blinked and her gaze met Tom's. "Ahh… what?"

"Focus."

"I was."

"Really?"

Ellie smiled. Well, on the reason why she'd wanted a photo of him. He really was heart-skip-a-beat gorgeous and he was standing in her bedroom. Pity. "Why's the answer so important to you?"

"I don't like being lied to."

"Then why are you still here? And don't tell me because you want to know the truth. I already told you and you're still here. I think this is a bit obsessive even for you."

Tom stared at her a moment longer before he strode to the bedroom door and pulled it open. Ellie stared after him in surprise. She hurried into the kitchen in time to hear him snap at his brother.

"Let's go, Sam."

Sam waved towards the dishes in the sink. "I haven't cleaned up yet."

Ellie looked at Sam. Those dishes certainly hadn't been dirty earlier. "What-"

Sam interrupted her. "Sorry. I cook when… that is… there's a cake in the oven. Take it out when the timer goes. You'll need more strawberry jam. The jar's nearly empty."

"Cake?" Ellie stared at him incredulously. "Where did you get the ingredients from?"

"You bought eggs and milk today." He shrugged. "There was sugar and flour in the cupboard and butter in the fridge."

"That's it? That's all you need for a cake?" Ellie looked from Sam to the stove.

He nodded, shrugged uncertainly and then glanced at his brother. "Flavour. I used the strawberry jam. I've got to go." He hurried towards the front door.

When Tom started to follow his brother, Ellie grabbed his arm. She checked Sam was outside before she spoke softly. "What just happened?"

"Don't hurt my brother." Tom pulled away from her and followed Sam to the car.

"I've stepped into an alternate universe," Ellie muttered before she followed them. She reached the car as Tom started it. She rapped on the passenger window and waited for it to open. "Thank you. For the cake." She smiled at Sam.

"Wednesday? Are you coming to dinner?" Sam asked.

Why did he have to have puppy dog eyes? "Ahh… sure. Why not?"

"You don't have to," Sam said. "I mean you don't have to feel like you have to."

Ellie shook her head. "A free meal. What's not to like?"

Sam turned to Tom. "Can you pick Beth up?"

"It's Ellie. And only if she can be ready at six."

Sam turned back to her. "I think you're more a Beth than an Ellie. See you Wednesday." He smiled before he pressed the button to close the window.

Ellie waved as they drove off, feeling confused. She slowly turned and walked back inside. "What have I got myself into?"

She was still asking herself the same question Wednesday night, when six o'clock was rapidly approaching, as she stared at the clothes hanging in her wardrobe. She glanced at the time on her alarm clock again. Only nineteen minutes until Tom arrived. She ran her hands across the clothes, shifting them slightly as she did. Nothing seemed right. All she could picture was the immaculate lounge room and the frosty reception Teresa had first given her. She glanced at the time again. Eighteen minutes. She jumped when someone knocked on the front door.

Chapter Ten

Ellie peered out her window, which faced the verandah. She swore when she saw Tom standing impatiently by the front door. Tightening the sash on her dressing gown, she hurried to the front door as he knocked on it again. She tugged at her hem, wishing it went below mid thigh. Ellie held the door half open and stared at Tom.

"You're early."

"Are you going to make me stand on the doorstep while I wait for you or are you going to let me in?"

Ellie stepped out of the doorway, trying to ignore the anger she heard in his tone. "I've only got to get dressed and then I'm ready."

Tom looked at the watch he wore tonight. "You've got fifteen minutes."

Ellie considered a few comebacks but discarded them. She wasn't going to start the night off with a fight. It looked like that was all Tom was interested in. Instead, she nodded and headed back to her bedroom. She pulled a dress off a hanger and threw her dressing gown on the bed, pulling the dress over her head. It was a soft yellow with thin straps and a full skirt that nearly reached her knees. She pulled on a pair of sandals with a low heel, touched up her lipstick and grabbed her small handbag. Dropping her lipstick in her handbag, along with her mobile phone, she locked her room behind her.

She held his gaze a moment before she spoke. "I'm ready."

Tom moved towards her, his gaze travelling from her head to her feet and back again. "So I see."

Once again Ellie discarded the first comment that came to mind. No stirring up trouble, she reminded herself. "I can't wait to eat what your brother's making for dinner. That cake he made was unbelievable. I couldn't believe it came out of ingredients I had lying around the house."

"Don't mention it in front of our mother." Tom stared at her for a moment before he strode to the front door.

Ellie hurried after him. She hadn't seen either of them at school the last two days so she hadn't been able to thank Sam yet. He also hadn't been online.

She locked the front door behind her, leaving the verandah light on. "What's wrong with her knowing?"

Tom held the passenger door open for her. "Were you hoping for the truth or would you like me to spin you some bullshit like you do for me?"

"Oh forget it." Ellie dropped into the car seat and stared straight ahead. She jumped slightly when Tom slammed the door. A heavy sigh escaped and she wondered if she should've said no to dinner. But she hadn't been able to. Sam had let her stay an entire weekend without questions, fed her and tried to entertain her. She hadn't had the heart to say no when faced with his hopeful expression.

Tom slid into the driver's seat and started the car. "If it comes up, I invited you."

"Why?"

"Because the rule in the house is no dating until seventeen."

"But I'm not dating your brother."

"My mother believes males and females can't be friends."

"At all?"

"There are a few exceptions."

Ellie was suddenly thinking the night mightn't be

too bad after all. Or at least it should be interesting. "Like what?"

"If you're gay or with someone else. But then she usually follows that up by saying that gay doesn't stop you from being bi and having a partner doesn't stop you from sleeping around on them."

Ellie grinned. "Does that mean I've got to pretend to be gay or in a relationship?"

"No."

"Or...." She looked Tom up and down. "Maybe she's expecting me to be dating you, since you supposedly invited me." Was this why he was angry?

Tom glanced over his shoulder and pulled up on the side of the road. He drew on the handbrake and pushed the gear stick into neutral. "Are you planning on making problems tonight?"

"Are you looking for a fight tonight?"

"Quit doing that. Just answer the question I asked."

Ellie shook her head. "No. Now how about you answer my question."

Tom leaned back in his seat and temporarily closed his eyes. "Probably."

"Why?"

Tom turned back to face her. A streetlight streamed in the windscreen of the car leaving half his face in shadows. "My brother has two friends and they're both geekier than he is. Why are you even talking to my brother let alone hanging out with him?"

Ellie's first instinct was to lie, and then she thought what the hell, he reckoned he wanted the truth. "I don't know. Well, actually, I sort of do. He's really weird and sometimes he completely creeps me out. Then he goes and does something sweet like baking me a divine cake. But even with all that, I don't know if I'd be here tonight if it wasn't for you."

Tom stared at her several minutes before he reached out and cupped her cheek. He ran his thumb across her skin as he continued to stare at her. Ellie moved forward impatiently, her lips meeting his. His hand slid behind her head and Ellie's hands reached for him. One went round his waist, the other rested high on his chest. Minutes passed before Tom pulled away slightly.

Ellie smiled up at him. "I hate bucket seats."

Tom stared at her for a split second before he laughed. "I think I might too." He swiftly kissed her again before he let her go and leaned back in his seat. He released the handbrake and put the car into gear.

Ellie continued to smile as they drove. When they got closer to their destination, she pulled out her lipstick and repaired the damage. She glanced over to Tom who laughed softly. "What?"

He shook his head as he pulled up in front of his house.

"Tell me."

"I was just wondering if I should make that a waste of your time."

Ellie grinned. "And your conclusion?"

"Anticipation improves everything."

Ellie laughed as Tom hopped out. She was waiting beside the car when he reached her side. Locking the car, he took her hand, entwining his fingers in hers. They were nearly at the front door when Ellie stopped and tugged on his hand.

Tom turned towards her. "What?"

"Do you have a girlfriend?" When he shook his head she frowned. "Why not?"

"Don't sound disappointed."

"I'm not. But well, you don't look like you've got a lack of girls chasing you."

Tom grinned. "Was that a compliment?"

"Okay, fine. Answering a question with a question is an annoying and irritating habit. Now please answer me properly."

"We broke up a couple of weeks ago because I

refused to go to a party with her instead of a swim meet."

Before Ellie had a chance to reply, the front door opened and Sam stood there. Tom strode towards the house, pulling Ellie with him. She reluctantly entered the front door. Slipping off her sandals, she left them lined up with the other shoes already there, waiting for Tom to remove his shoes.

"Hi, Beth." Sam smiled shyly.

"Ahh… hi." Ellie glanced at Tom.

Tom rolled his eyes. "You make her sound like she has a multiple personality disorder."

Ellie grinned. "Don't worry. It's Lizzie who's the crazy one."

"Well let me know when she's about and I'll hide the knives," Tom said.

"Nah, you only have to hide the knives when Lisbeth is about." Ellie glanced around, looking for Teresa. "Where's your mum?"

"In the study," Sam said.

Ellie relaxed, coming further into the house. "I wanted to thank you for the cake. You're an absolute genius in the kitchen. I shared it with Lauren. She said if you're not careful she'll kidnap you and chain you to her kitchen and make you cook food like that for her every day."

Sam blushed. "It was only a cake," he mumbled.

Ellie shook her head. "Nah-uh. We decided each slice was a piece of heaven."

"Leave him alone." Tom draped his arm around her shoulders. "It's not nice to torment your host."

"I'm not tormenting. Seriously. Lauren told me if I don't bring her something just as delicious tomorrow I'll be sitting on my own for lunch."

Sam's face went even redder before he mumbled, "I better check dinner."

Tom pulled her towards him, wrapping his arms loosely around her waist. "That wasn't very nice."

Ellie draped her arms around his neck and smiled. "That was me being nice."

"Then you better warn me when you let Lisbeth loose. I don't think we'll live through it."

Ellie chuckled. When Tom's head lowered, she said, "I thought you mentioned something about anticipation?"

"You just don't want me to wreck your lipstick."

Ellie grinned. "That too." A sound behind her had her turning her head. She tried to pull away from Tom when she saw his mother coming towards them.

Tom kept one arm around her. "Mum, you remember Beth?"

Teresa nodded. "The actress."

"That was the last day. I don't think I'll do any more acting. It was much harder than I expected it to be."

"Oh, I don't know. I think you're a natural," Tom said.

Ellie grinned. "Thank you."

Sam joined them again. "Dinner's ready."

The four of them wandered over to the table and Sam gestured to seats as he said each of their names. As soon as they were all seated, Sam served. Ellie could barely wait for Sam to join them at the table so she could start eating. The smells made her mouth water. As soon as someone else started to eat, she began.

"What's this called?" Ellie gestured towards the meal with her fork.

"Cajun crawfish and shrimp etouffe."

Ellie stared at him. "Shrimp what?"

"Eh-too-fay." Sam said the word slowly.

"I've never heard of it in my life, but it tastes wonderful."

"It's an authentic Louisiana recipe."

"Ahh... okay." She didn't know much about Louisiana, but after tonight she could say that their food was awesome.

The meal was mostly quiet, with a few easy

questions from Teresa. Following the main meal they had chocolate strawberry shortcake for dessert. Teresa excused herself, the moment dinner was ended, to return to her study. Ellie offered to help clean up but Sam sent her and Tom to the downstairs lounge room.

Ellie dropped onto the double seater lounge. "I don't think I could eat another bite. I feel like I'm about to explode."

Tom joined her. "Who was the one who asked for seconds of dessert?"

Ellie grinned. "You saw what I eat each week. How could I resist a second helping of dessert?"

Tom put his arm around her shoulder and pulled her closer. "When do you have to be home?"

"Ahh…"

"You don't, do you?"

"Well…"

"You want to give me the real story about last weekend?"

Ellie sighed. "Don't wreck such a perfect night."

"Are you ever planning to tell me?"

Ellie stared at him for several minutes. It had been so much easier to lie to him when she didn't really know him. "I don't know."

"Thank you."

"What for?"

Tom grinned. "For actually telling me the truth."

"If I wasn't too full to move, I'd protest that by sitting in the chair furthest from you."

"Did you realise you've got no lipstick left on now?"

"Really? And you thought it was important to point that out because?"

Tom's lips met hers in answer. They were still on the couch making out when Sam clattered down the stairs. Ellie pulled away from Tom, but he kept his arm around her and wouldn't let her move far. He shook his head at the query on her face.

Chapter Eleven

Sam held out a plastic container with two slices of shortcake in it. "For you and Lauren tomorrow. It'd probably be best to sit it on an ice brick and wrap it up in a tea towel to keep it from getting too warm in your schoolbag."

"Thanks."

"You said she wouldn't sit with you for lunch."

"Ahh… I think she was only threatening. I don't think she really meant it. Although we are talking about your cooking. So maybe she might have."

"Thanks for coming tonight."

"Ahh… sure."

"I'll…" Sam gestured towards his room. "Well…"

Ellie pulled away from Tom so she could sit up properly. "We didn't get through all those movies on the weekend. Did you want to watch one of them now?"

Sam glanced behind himself, towards the time displayed on the DVD player. "I only have half an hour before I have to go to bed."

"Oh."

"I can watch the start of it with you," Sam offered.

"Only if you don't have anything else you wanted to do before you head to bed."

Sam shook his head. "Which one did you want to watch? They're still down here."

Ellie shrugged. She couldn't remember which movies she'd picked out. "Surprise me."

Tom pulled her back against him and she rested her head on his shoulder as Sam put the movie on. When Sam went to bed, the movie was forgotten. Ellie willingly kissed Tom, her hands roaming as freely as his. The movie returning to the menu reminded them of their surroundings.

Tom smiled. "I should probably give you a lift home. I've got to get up early in the morning."

"I guess."

"You don't sound all that enthusiastic. Were you planning on staying again? There's plenty of space in my bed."

Ellie stared at him for a moment. "On the weekend, when I asked which bedroom was mine, why did you say yours?"

"You were making my brother uncomfortable. So what do you say? Are you staying?"

Ellie laughed softly. "No thanks. You'd still be complaining in the morning that you needed more sleep. And no way am I getting up that early. I get out of bed as late as possible. I usually barely make it to school on time."

"We better move then before I start trying to talk you into staying."

Ellie reluctantly pulled away from Tom. She picked up the container Sam had given her and waited for Tom to turn off the television. They crept quietly upstairs and when they reached the foyer, Ellie carried her sandals so she didn't risk making too much noise as she walked out the door. All the lights, except for the foyer light, were turned off. She wondered if Teresa had gone to bed already. Tom slipped his shoes on before he headed outside, locking the door behind him.

Ellie found the drive went too quickly and they were pulling up in front of her house before she was ready to say goodnight. "Have you been at school the past couple of days?"

Tom nodded.

"I didn't see either of you about."

"We were there. But I could say the same. Where were you?"

"I sit in the same place every lunchtime." She described where the tree was that she and Lauren had been sitting under since grade eight.

"I know where that is."

"Does that mean I might see you tomorrow?"

Tom leaned forward and kissed her. "Maybe."

Ellie smiled. "Goodnight."

"Night, Beth."

She considered questioning his choice of names but the faint look of amusement told her he waited for exactly that. She grinned and hopped out of the car, still holding the container. Dashing to the front door, she turned and waved to him before she let herself in. She heard him drive off as soon as the door was closed.

Ellie hid the container in the back of the fridge and, still smiling, made her way to her room. The house was quiet and dark. She knew her mum would be home and probably asleep, but she felt like she was the only one in the house. Locking her door behind her, she turned on the light and changed into her sleepwear.

* * *

Ellie reached for her phone, her eyes still tightly shut. She cracked an eye open to check the time before she read the message. *What time do you leave for school?* She groaned. There was still another forty-five minutes she could be sleeping. It only took fifteen minutes to get ready. If that.

Still sleeping- Lisbeth.

Knives hidden. What time?

Ellie considered ignoring him, but didn't think he'd stop sending messages. She thought it best to reply. *Eight.*

She glared at the phone. When it remained silent she went back to sleep to be woken, what felt like minutes later, by her alarm clock. She hit snooze and considered waiting until it went off again. But if she did, it wouldn't give her enough time to get to school before classes started. Turning off her alarm, she staggered out of bed.

By the time she was ready to leave, it was five past eight. As she stepped out the front door, she froze. Tom was parked on the side of the road, waiting for her. Sam sat in the back seat and Tom leaned against the bonnet of his car. When he saw her, he strode up the cracked path, meeting her on the edge of the verandah.

He glanced at the piece of buttered toast she held. "Is that your breakfast?"

Ellie grinned. "I was tempted to have chocolate strawberry shortcake. You'd be amazed at how much willpower I needed to use."

"You'll be hungry before you finish your first class."

Ellie shook her head. "I've got an apple in my bag. Anyway, I'm old enough to feed myself without any help at all."

"You forget. I saw what you buy and call food." Tom took her schoolbag.

"We can't all have a chef for a brother." Ellie grinned at Sam as they reached the car. "Hi, Sam." She noticed his gaze went to her toast too. "And don't start about my breakfast. Considering how many fires I've caused in kitchens, toast is the safest thing for me to make."

"I wasn't going to say anything." Sam held out a container.

Ellie took it and peeked inside. She grinned. "You are absolutely wonderful."

"I wasn't sure if you'd manage to keep the pieces I gave you last night."

"It was close." Ellie sat in the car, quickly finished off her toast and then slowly ate the shortcake Sam had given her.

"I swear that food is getting more attention than I got." Tom started the car.

"If you had chocolate drizzled all over you I might give you the same amount of attention." Ellie took another bite.

"I'll have to keep that in mind."

Ellie looked over at him, startled by his answer. Then she laughed. "Okay, fair enough. But don't expect me to think clearly until I've been awake at least an hour. Anything I say before then I maintain the right to take back."

"So what time will that be today?"

"About fifteen minutes before school starts." Ellie licked her fingers and frowned at the container. She could have eaten a piece twice that size. "I'm going to end up as big as a house if I keep hanging out with you two."

"You could always join me in the pool each morning."

Ellie shuddered theatrically. "Just because you're crazy enough to get up at that hour doesn't mean I will be."

Sam took the container back. "It's not too bad."

"Don't tell me you go swimming with him."

Sam shrugged. "Not every day. And just for the fun of it. I don't compete. I'm nowhere near fast enough."

Ellie shook her head. "You're both crazy."

"Don't knock something until you've tried it," Tom said.

They pulled up at school and Ellie looked around. "What are so many people doing here at this hour? It's still ages until school starts."

"Catching up." Tom hopped out of the car.

Ellie joined him. "With what?"

Tom rolled his eyes. "Friends."

"I'd rather catch up on sleep."

Tom locked his car the moment Sam was out of it. "Who did you send the photo to?"

Ellie frowned. "Huh?"

"When I was swimming."

She grinned. "No one. Well, I did send it, but I sent it to my email address. And there were two of them." She pulled out her phone, flicked through her gallery and showed him. "See, nothing to panic about. You look gorgeous in both of them." She returned her phone to her pocket.

"Why did you take them?"

"Because you wouldn't let me take one when I said I was going to."

Tom draped his arm around her shoulder, taking her schoolbag. His was slung over his shoulder and he carried hers. "So what was that? Lizzie breaking free?"

"Probably."

Tom stopped and pulled her close, her bag dropping to the ground. "I like the way Lizzie kisses."

Ellie slowly smiled. "Really?"

Tom nodded before his lips met hers. He ignored the couple of catcalls and drew back from her when he was finished. "Really."

"What are you planning on doing now?"

"Catching up with friends. You coming?"

"Ahh… sure."

"There's no need to be nervous."

"I'm never nervous."

Tom smiled. "If you say so." He picked up her bag.

"Never."

"I'm not arguing."

Did he think she was an idiot? "Yes you are. With your tone."

"Okay, maybe not nervous. But at least uncomfortable."

"Maybe." Ellie smiled up at him. No one other than Lauren had ever noticed when she was uncomfortable or uncertain about a situation. She wasn't sure if she liked it. She glanced away. It might take a bit of getting used to.

Chapter Twelve

Ellie slowly opened the container with frequent glances at Lauren to see how she was handling the lengthy process. She grinned at the impatient look her friend gave her.

"If you don't hurry up I'm going to mug you and eat both pieces," Lauren warned.

Tom joined them in time to hear Lauren's comment. He laughed and his gaze met Ellie's. "Anticipation improves everything."

Ellie smiled back at him. "I seem to have heard that comment somewhere. I'm just not sure where."

Tom sat down beside her and whispered in her ear. "Liar."

Ellie finally opened the container and offered it to Lauren so she could choose a piece. "You might as well take the biggest piece. I've had three so far."

"Not fair." Lauren took a bite out of her piece. "Ohh. This is to kill for."

"Isn't the comment usually to die for?" Tom asked.

"Nope, that's Ellie's line when I take the second piece from her."

"Dream on." Ellie took as big a bite as she possibly could.

"What are you doing this weekend?" Tom asked.

Ellie had to finish her mouthful before she could answer. "Going to my father's place. Why?"

"I was just wondering if you wanted to go to a party with me tomorrow night."

"Sorry. Maybe next time."

Tom nodded.

"Hey, Tom! I've been looking all over for you."

"Dale. This is Ellie and her friend Lauren." Tom looked first to Ellie and then over to Lauren.

"Hey." Dale smiled at each of them before he turned back to Tom. "We're having a quick game of basketball. You interested?"

Ellie smiled at Tom when he turned towards her. "Go on. It'll give us time to talk about you behind your back. Although I've got a feeling that'll only be after we've raved about your brother's cooking."

"Good thing I don't have a self esteem problem."

Tom's lips met hers before he rose to his feet. "I'll meet you at my car after school."

Ellie nodded and watched as Tom walked off with Dale.

Lauren scooted over to sit closer to her, nudging her in the ribs. "I swear I can't leave you alone for five minutes without your life completely changing. Now tell me everything. If you leave out a single detail I swear I'll never speak to you again."

Ellie grinned. "Not every little detail, surely."

"You didn't!" Lauren exclaimed.

Ellie kept silent for a few seconds before she relented and shook her head. "Nah. But I was so tempted to stay the night. Isn't he just melt-in-a-puddle gorgeous?"

"How did you end up together?"

"I'm still trying to figure that one out myself."

"Then tell me everything and I'll help you work it out."

Ellie laughed. "You just want to hear all about my night."

Lauren grinned. "Yep. But I'll use my amazing powers of deduction to help you discover exactly what went on in exchange for all the details."

"Hmm, where do I start?"

"Oh, hurry up. Lunchtime will be over before I get to hear anything."

Ellie smiled. There were some things she didn't want to share, even with Lauren. But that still left heaps she could tell her about.

* * *

She swung the front door open, her schoolbag slung over her shoulder. Through the doorway she could see Tom's car parked out the front. She smiled when he walked around the front of his car, stopping at the edge of the footpath. Behind her the phone rang. With a wave, she turned away to answer the phone, dropping her bag on the floor. "Yeah?"

"Elizabeth?"

"Dad." She should have known it was him. He was about the only person who rang on the landline.

"I'm glad I caught you, Elizabeth."

She stilled. He had that tone, the one he used when he was about to tell her something she wouldn't like. "What's wrong?"

"Well, I know this is short notice…"

"Something else has come up, hasn't it?"

"I'd rather have you visit. Maybe the next weekend. Ahh, hold on a minute."

Ellie waited as her father covered the mouthpiece of the phone and had a muffled conversation. She guessed it was with Pamela. And she bet she was saying the following weekend was out. She wasn't about to give Pamela the satisfaction. "Hey, Dad."

"Yes?"

"Next weekend isn't any good for me. I think the following one might be out too. But I don't have my appointment diary in front of me." Appointment diary! Yeah right. That was something Pamela kept, not her.

"I'm sorry to hear that."

"I've got to go, Dad. Otherwise I'll be late to school."

"Goodbye, Elizabeth."

"Yeah. Bye."

She hung up the phone and dropped onto the floor to lean up against the wall. Closing her eyes, she tried not to think about anything. She hated Pamela. Not that she had really wanted to visit her father. She was always bored senseless every time she was there. It just annoyed her that Pamela always seemed to find a reason why she couldn't visit.

"Ellie?"

She opened her eyes to see Tom at the front door. For a moment she'd forgotten he was waiting for her.

She started to struggle to her feet and gritted her teeth when Tom came over to help her up. Brushing his hands away, she continued to sit on the floor instead. "Sorry. Phone call."

Tom sat on the floor next to her. "Bad news?"

"In a way." Ellie quickly came to a decision. "Do you still want me to go to that party tonight?"

"Yeah. Was that your father?"

Ellie nodded. "Yeah."

"What time would you have to be home?"

"Sunday."

"What's going on, Ellie?"

"Can we talk about it later?"

Tom shook his head. "I doubt you will."

"We can't leave Sam out in the car all morning."

"Stop procrastinating."

She looked away from Tom. Her words tumbled out, all running together. "My father left when I was thirteen and he married a woman my mum calls Stupid Bitch and she has two clones she claims are her daughters. That's what everyone thinks, anyway. What really happened was that Dad decided Mum needed help because she has a drinking problem. She went ballistic and threw him out and he tried to convince me to go with him. But I already knew

I'd be crazy to live with him. Mum has always been ahh… laid back."

"Okay, that sounds fairly straightforward. What has that got to do with you staying at my place on the weekend?"

She still couldn't look at Tom, but at least her words were no longer strung together. "Up until a few weeks ago I stayed at Lauren's every weekend. We sort of got into a little trouble together and she's not allowed to have anything more to do with me."

"Trouble?"

"We were caught sneaking back in from a party." She couldn't resist a glance towards him. "And stop grinning." She glared at him until he looked serious again. "Promise me you won't tell this to anyone?"

Tom took her hand. "I promise."

"Mum drinks a lot. Not so bad during the week. But by the time Friday arrives she's ready to kill for a drink. She starts about midday and doesn't stop until early Sunday morning when she passes out for most of the day. Her mates come over and they party all weekend. I just don't want to be here during her parties."

"Is that what the padlocks are for?"

Ellie nodded.

"Why don't you leave?"

"It mightn't be perfect, but I like this set up. I come and go as I please. I run the household how I want. My only other options are living with Dad, which I'm beginning to think mightn't be an option anymore thanks to Stupid Bitch, or boarding school. My father offered to send me to one about a year ago. And I certainly don't want to end up in a foster home again." She instantly regretted the last words she spoke, dropping her gaze to her hand in his.

"Is that why you don't live in a better neighbourhood?"

"Yeah." Maybe he hadn't realised the significance of her comment. She wasn't going to point it out if he hadn't.

"Why didn't you tell me, Ellie?"

"I barely knew you last weekend. I wasn't about to spill every family secret to you."

Tom smiled slightly. "Fair enough." He rose to his feet, helping her up. "Are you going to bring more clothes than you did last time? And swimmers?"

"I can stay?"

Tom nodded. "Of course you can."

"And you won't expect... ahh... that is-"

"I won't expect anything more than last weekend."

Ellie threw her arms around him. She'd already known he was different to Brody, but she'd needed to make certain. "Thank you. I'll only be a minute." She dashed back to her room and unlocked it. Grabbing the bag she'd packed to take to her father's, she shoved in her bikini and the black dress she'd worn last weekend. She hunted around for her high heels and shoved them in too. Locking her door behind her, she grinned. "Ready now."

"Good." Tom took her bags. "Let's go before we're late."

"I bet you've never been late to school in your life."

"Never. Now being on time to class, that's a different matter altogether."

Ellie laughed, suddenly able to look forward to the weekend again. And surprised to find she was actually relieved she didn't have to lie to Tom anymore.

Chapter Thirteen

Even though Ellie wore the same black dress and heels she had last weekend, the night was turning out completely different. She'd talked Tom into bringing Lauren, who planned to catch a taxi at eleven-thirty so she arrived home before her midnight curfew. Ellie thought it was completely crazy that Lauren's mother accepted her word on who she was with and where she was going. Yet couldn't trust Lauren to hang out with her. It didn't make any sense at all. But when did parents ever make sense? Hers were a perfect example of that.

She sighed when a song with a faster beat began and she started to draw away from Tom's arms. He smiled at her, pulling her back against him. She wasn't about to argue if he wanted to stay wrapped around her while everyone else picked up their dance pace. She was content to pretend the song was the slowest one ever written.

"You want another drink?" Tom whispered against her ear.

"Nah, better not." She grinned. "Or is that part of your plan?"

He laughed softly. "Looks like it must be close to eleven-thirty. Your friend's headed over this way."

Ellie turned in time to see Lauren before she hugged the two of them. "Are you leaving?"

Grinning, Lauren nodded. "Having the absolute best time. I don't want to leave, but I'm on probation so I better not be late. What are you doing tomorrow?"

"I don't know." Ellie turned to Tom.

"Other than swimming for a couple of hours in the morning, no plans." He turned to Lauren. "You're welcome to come over if you want."

Lauren nodded, still grinning. "As soon as I wake up. Directions?"

Tom explained how to find his place and told her to use the wooden gate beside the garage. He pulled Ellie back to him as soon as Lauren left.

The rest of the night seemed to fly and it was nearly three in the morning when Tom drove them back to his place. He pulled up in front of the house, turning the ignition off.

"What?" Ellie asked when he continued to stare at her.

"I'm trying to figure out if I have enough self control to kiss you when we're inside or if I should do it out here."

Ellie grinned. "If we're taking into account my self control, you'd better kiss me while we're in these stupid bucket seats."

Tom laughed softly before his lips met hers. Ellie didn't know how long they sat in the car, but she reluctantly let Tom go when their kiss ended.

"Time to go inside, unless you want to climb into the backseat with me," Tom said.

Ellie laughed. "That's a surprisingly tempting offer." She opened the car door, but remained sitting. "But if I don't get to bed soon I'll probably crash here."

"Does that mean you'd say yes if you weren't tired?"

"Not at all." She grinned.

"That's what I thought." Tom hopped out of the car and joined her on the footpath. Once he locked the car, he slipped his arm around her waist. "You can have the bathroom first."

"Thanks dear." She grinned when Tom laughed. "I couldn't resist. It just sounded so domestic."

Tom opened the wooden gate. "Try and keep the noise down. My parents are both home."

"Would they kick me out?"

"I don't know." Tom shut the gate behind them.

"Why not?"

"Because you're my first girlfriend that's stayed the night." Tom unlocked the door. "I've only been seventeen for a bit over a month. And don't bother with the question you're about to ask."

"How do you know what I was going to ask?" Ellie blinked when Tom turned on the light.

He smiled. "I have a fair idea. You're always full of questions. Now hurry up and use the bathroom. I'd like to get to bed before daylight."

* * *

Ellie reluctantly opened her eyes. She didn't move. She was far too comfortable. Her back was pressed against Tom's chest and his arm was over her waist. She smiled and her eyes started to close again. Then she heard it again. This time she sat up, disturbing Tom.

"What are you doing?" he mumbled, reaching out to pull her back to him.

"I thought I heard Lauren."

Tom glanced at the alarm clock. "It's not even eight. You're imagining things."

"There. Did you hear that?"

"It'll be Sam playing online. I bet he's hooked it up to a speaker and mic instead of a headset. I'll kill him. Later though. After I've finished sleeping."

Ellie shook her head and clambered over Tom. "Go back to sleep. I won't be able to until I see for myself."

Tom groaned. "Fine. I need at least another hour's sleep." He rolled onto his stomach, pulling a pillow over his head.

Ellie smiled as she watched him. The sheet was pooled around his waist, his bare back tempting her to run her hands over his tanned skin. Another shout from the lounge room had her moving. She opened the door and stared at Sam and Lauren. They both wore headsets. Only Sam had a controller.

Lauren leapt to her feet and pointed at the television. "Red dot on your back. They've snuck up behind you. Don't let them kill you. Yes! Brilliant."

On the screen, Sam's character spun and shot the man that had been sneaking up on him. Sam grinned.

"I'd seen you before Lauren spoke. Face it, I always kick your arse at this game."

Lauren laughed. "So what excuse do you use when I'm not here?"

Ellie guessed they were talking to someone only they could hear on the headsets. Closing the door, she moved further into the lounge room and saw two plates on the floor. Both were empty. Her stomach grumbled and she wondered what Sam had made to eat. She was halfway across the room before Lauren noticed her.

Lauren removed her headset, bent close to Sam to whisper in his ear and then hurried to Ellie's side. "I was wondering when you were going to wake up. Half the day is gone."

"Not everyone has an unnatural liking for early mornings like you do." Ellie glanced towards the bathroom. "Give me a minute." When she returned to the lounge room, Sam was turning his game off.

He looked over to Ellie. "Breakfast?"

"Are you cooking?"

"Sort of."

Ellie frowned. "That doesn't sound good."

"I'll teach you how to make pancakes."

Lauren put her hand on Sam's shoulder. They were

the same height. "I don't know if anyone has warned you what Ellie is like in the kitchen."

Sam nodded. "I won't let her burn the place down."

Ellie worried at her lip with her teeth. "Ahh… well… I don't know."

"Is the place insured?" Lauren asked.

Sam nodded. "Don't you want to learn, Beth?"

Ellie shook her head, nodded and then frowned. "I want to learn. I just don't want to burn the place down in the process."

"You won't. Come on." Sam headed for the stairs.

Ellie and Lauren looked at each other, shrugged then followed him. When they reached the top of the stairs, Lauren froze.

Lauren stared, eyes wide in surprise. "Wow. You were right about the 'keep off the carpet' sign. I guess they forgot to put it out. I thought you must have been exaggerating when you told me."

Ellie grinned, linked her arm through Lauren's and took her to the kitchen. "You can see why I'm worried about burning the place down."

"A lot of stainless steel in here. That doesn't catch fire," Lauren said.

Sam placed a bowl on the bench. "Wash your hands." He continued to pull out ingredients and utensils as they obeyed.

By the time the batter was mixed and they waited for the first pancake to cook, Ellie smiled at Sam. "This is surprisingly fun." She dipped her finger in the batter and popped it in her mouth.

"Hey!" Lauren protested. "We've all got to eat that."

Ellie held the bowl out to Lauren and grinned when her friend dipped her own finger in. "Tastes good, doesn't it?" She squealed when arms went round her waist and she nearly dropped the mixture.

Sam rescued the bowl, returning it to the bench. "No wonder things catch on fire. You get distracted too easily." He flipped the pancake.

Ellie turned in Tom's arms, sliding her hands across his chest to link them behind his head. "I thought you were going to sleep for an hour."

He whispered against her ear, "I missed you." He pressed his lips on the pulse point below her ear.

"I'm meant to be having a cooking lesson," Ellie said as his lips moved to hers.

Tom looked past Ellie before his gaze met hers again. "Trust me, you're not being missed."

Ellie was about to look and see what he meant when his lips met hers. Then she couldn't have cared what Sam and Lauren were doing. She opened her mouth, pressing herself against Tom. Time became meaningless and the kitchen faded. When they finally broke apart, Sam was setting the table and Lauren had taken over flipping pancakes. She grinned when Ellie looked towards her.

Ellie suddenly frowned and turned back to Tom. "Where are your parents?"

Tom laughed. "You weren't very concerned about that question before."

"You did tell me not to wake them last night."

Tom nodded. "They left about seven this morning. Well, I assume they did since they told us that's what time they planned to leave."

"When will they be back?"

"This afternoon. Why? Did you want to make use of their spa bath?"

Ellie stared at him. "You're kidding me, right?"

Tom shook his head. "Do you want to see?"

Ellie hesitated. "Ahh… yeah?"

Tom grinned, taking her hand. "Come on then."

Ellie stood in the doorway of the ensuite. It was nearly as big as her entire bedroom. In one corner was the spa bath, a shower in the corner opposite and a vanity with two sinks ran along the wall across from the door. The toilet had its own separate area.

Tom's arms went around her and he pulled her

back against his chest. His chin rested on her shoulder. "What do you say? Want to try it out?"

Ellie met his gaze in the mirror above the vanity. She didn't know if she should take him seriously or not. Especially with the way he grinned at her. "Maybe another day. I believe I was promised a swim."

"Chicken," Tom said softly.

Ellie laughed. "You'll have to do better than that to make me change my mind." When he turned her in his arms and started to kiss her again, she was more than tempted. She was relieved when Lauren yelled from the kitchen.

"Breakfast is served!"

Ellie pulled away from him. "Looks like I just got a better offer."

He walked with her back to the kitchen. "I'm beginning to learn that nothing can compete against food in your eyes."

"And people say you can't teach old dogs new tricks."

Tom rolled his eyes. "All these compliments are going to have me dragging you back to bed."

"Not before I've eaten my share of pancakes." Ellie sat at the table.

"Of course not. I wouldn't dream about getting

between you and food. I'd be terrified for my life." Tom put a pancake in his bowl.

"Only good food." Ellie waited for Lauren to finish helping herself to the ice cream before she piled some on her pancake.

"Considering what your diet is like at home, I'm going to be sensible and let you feed first," Tom said.

Lauren handed the maple syrup to Ellie. "Smart move. That'd also mean she'll be too well fed to put up much of a fight."

Ellie forgot all about talking when she had her first bite of breakfast. Her eyes closed and she moaned.

Lauren laughed. "It's good. Maybe not as good as you're acting it is."

"Shh. Sacrilege." Ellie had another mouthful.

Sam divided his time between watching Ellie and Lauren. He remained quiet as Ellie, Lauren and Tom carried the conversation. Once breakfast was finished, Sam cleaned up while the three of them returned to the lounge room downstairs.

Lauren flopped onto the couch. "I think I ate too much."

Ellie brought the beanbag out of Sam's room and dropped it onto the floor. "Tell me about it." She lay back on the beanbag, wriggling to get comfortable.

"Does this mean no one's up for a swim yet?" Tom

sat on the floor, leaning against the lounge chair closest to Ellie. He linked his fingers through hers.

"Does it involve moving from this spot?" Ellie closed her eyes and sighed heavily.

"What about this afternoon?" Tom asked.

"Sounds good. But you don't have to wait for us. I know you've got to train," Ellie said.

Tom brought her hand to his lips. He smiled slightly. "I'll wait."

Sam entered the room, noisily tripping on the last couple of steps. "Are we going swimming now?"

Lauren giggled. "We're all busy collapsing. Any ideas on something unenergetic we can do?"

Tom grinned. "Sam's first thought is always computer games."

"Sounds good to me. How about teams. Sam and I against you two," Lauren said.

"Only because you know he's the best player," Ellie said.

"Why would I want to be on the losing team?" Lauren asked.

Ellie laughed. "Someone better give me a controller if they want me to play. I'm not moving for any reason."

Chapter Fourteen

The morning passed rapidly. Ellie was surprised the game was fun when they all played. Sam put together a salad for lunch and late afternoon found them heading for the pool.

Ellie and Lauren were last to walk outside. When they rounded the corner of the house and could see Tom and Sam, Lauren clutched Ellie's arm and they came to a stop.

The boys dived into the water, swimming for the opposite end. Lauren's free hand covered her heart.

"Did you see them?"

Ellie nodded. "Can you understand why I stared at him when he was in a towel?"

"Forget about Tom. What about Sam? I bet if the kids at school ever saw him without his shirt they wouldn't be calling him Baby Face."

"Well…" Ellie watched as they surfaced, grinning

at each other. Tom splashed water at Sam who ducked back under the water. "You can't exactly argue that comment. He does have a really young face."

"But those muscles." Lauren shook Ellie's arm that she still clutched. "What about those muscles? You can call me shallow. I don't care. But please hand me a tissue to wipe off the drool."

"What about the creepy stare?"

"He forgets to do that when he's occupied. Like when he's cooking or playing games."

"You can't spend all your time cooking or playing computer games."

"Can't I?"

Ellie looked at her friend in surprise. "You like him?"

Lauren shrugged. "I don't know. He's odd. But when he forgets to be self-conscious he's actually pretty funny. You should have heard him talking to his mates online earlier. I was in stitches half the time."

"Yeah, but…" Ellie's voice trailed off when the brothers climbed out of the pool again.

Lauren grinned. "Did you forget what you were going to say?"

Ellie laughed. "You could say that. Uh-oh. That doesn't look good."

Tom and Sam started to walk towards them, grinning.

"I bet they're planning on throwing us in," Lauren whispered.

"Can't throw us in if we're already in the water." Ellie glanced at Lauren who nodded. They ran towards Tom and Sam, dodging to the side at the last second. When they reached the edge of the pool, they jumped in, breaking the surface grinning. Seconds later, Tom and Sam dived into the water with them.

Ellie tread water, watching Tom swim over to her. "So what did you pair think you were going to do?"

"You looked like you were having trouble making it to the pool. We were just going to give you a hand." Tom reached out to grab hold of the pool edge and pulled Ellie to him.

"We were a little distracted."

"By?"

Ellie ran a hand down Tom's chest and smiled. "I wouldn't like to say. I wouldn't want you to get an over inflated ego."

Tom's lips met hers. "Really? Are you planning on ending the conversation just when it's getting interesting?"

"Yep."

"I'm sure I could make you talk."

Ellie grinned, certain he meant by kissing her. "Do your worst." She squealed when he started to tickle her instead. "Okay. Okay! I'll talk."

Tom pulled her close. "So what was the distraction?"

"You. I was busy telling Lauren that you are burn-the-picture-in-your-retina gorgeous."

Tom laughed. "That good, hey?"

"You don't need me to tell you. I'm sure you already know."

"And I'm sure you don't need me to tell you the same. Unless you're playing at being the bride of Frankenstein."

"You're going to have to pay for that comment." Ellie tugged Tom's arm so he lost his grip on the side of the pool, pressing against his shoulders to make him go under. Spinning away, she started to swim to the other side of the pool. She doubted she'd reach her destination before he caught her. He'd already been getting over her surprise attack when she'd spun away from him.

She felt a hand wrap around her ankle, pulling her back. Tom held her close to him and she barely had time to take a deep breath before they sank under the water. His lips met hers. They kissed until they needed to surface for air.

Grinning, Ellie tread water. "I thought the whole idea of getting in the pool was for you to practise."

"Are you going to swim a couple of laps with me?"

Ellie shook her head. "I've got no chance of keeping up with you."

"So I'll keep up with you." Tom grinned. "Come on. Just two laps. What do you say?"

"Sure. Why not?"

After the two laps, Ellie stayed in the shallow end, reclining on the steps. Lauren joined her while Sam did laps with his brother. She watched Tom for a while, fascinated by the way his body moved through the water. She turned to Lauren to see her watching too.

"Which one?"

Lauren frowned as she glanced at Ellie. "Huh?"

"Who are you watching?"

"Sam. You know when you're little and you have an Easter egg hunt?"

"Yeah?" Ellie dragged the word out, uncertain what her friend was trying to say.

"And at the end of it you're left with a handful of chocolate eggs, all wrapped in different colours, looking pretty much the same other than the different clothes."

"Clothes?"

"Play along."

"Okay." Ellie drew the word out, shaking her head. "Easter eggs dressed in different coloured shirts. Then what?"

Lauren giggled. "Now you've got me picturing them with buttons down the front and empty sleeves 'cause they don't have arms."

Ellie rolled her eyes. "We're getting off track. What has this to do with Sam?"

"Well, you open up one of those little eggs and take a bite and it's chocolate, all the way through. Absolutely delicious."

"Of course. Chocolate always is." Ellie nodded.

"You have another one. Yummy, creamy chocolate."

"Yeah." Again Ellie drew the word out.

"Then you unwrap the next one and take a bite expecting to find chocolate and your mouth is filled with caramel as well."

"Are you meant to be going somewhere with this? Because you're starting to make me hungry."

Lauren laughed. "Just saying the word food makes you hungry. But yeah, I'm going somewhere. Sam's like that. He's not what you expect when you start to peel away the layers."

"Are we talking his body or his personality?"

"Well, I certainly can't ignore that body." Lauren grinned. "But I was including his personality in that too."

"What were you pair up to in the kitchen when Tom and I were a little oblivious to the rest of the world?"

"A little?" Lauren looked sceptical.

"Okay. Completely and utterly oblivious to the rest of the world."

"I rode over here this morning on my bike. Sam said he'd ride home with me this afternoon when it's time for me to go. I said it'd take about an hour. I was worried he might collapse along the way. I mean, he doesn't come across as a very active person. But he said that wasn't a problem. He often goes riding with his brother for a few hours at a time."

"Tom seems to love sport. All sport," Ellie said.

"Yeah, well I asked Sam if he played any sport and he said he wasn't really interested. He seems pretty fit considering he's not interested in playing sport. I got the feeling he joins his brother in things because they're friends."

Ellie watched the brothers as they kept pace with

each other. She smiled as she recalled Tom keeping pace with her. "Yeah, I think they are too."

"You know what?"

Ellie looked over to Lauren. "What?"

"We haven't played Marco Polo for ages."

"I'm guessing you're not talking the version we played in primary school?"

Lauren grinned. "What do you say? Think we can round up two blindfolds? I'm interested to see how keen Sam is to catch me when the prize is a kiss."

Ellie laughed. "You're just keen to see what he kisses like without committing yourself to anything. Just in case he kisses worse than a puppy."

"So? Sue me."

"I'm guessing I'm the one who has to suggest the game."

Lauren rolled her eyes. "What do you think? You're the one who spends half her time attached at the lips with Tom. And you better be persuasive, particularly when I'm reluctant."

"The things I'm called on to do in the name of friendship." Ellie grinned.

"Well?"

"Of course."

Ellie was glad they'd finished their game of Marco

Polo when Teresa came out on the patio and called to Tom.

Tom waved to his mother to let her know he heard her and swam over to the side of the pool, closest to the patio. Sam followed him. Ellie and Lauren shared a look before they swam over too.

"I was just letting you know we're home," Teresa called down when Tom and Sam were out of the pool.

"Mum, this is Beth's friend, Lauren." Tom gestured towards them as they pulled themselves out of the pool.

Ellie guessed she should probably tell Teresa that she was going by the name Ellie now. Although she wondered if it really mattered since Sam still called her Beth.

"Hello again, Beth. Lauren."

Ellie said hi at the same time as Lauren said hello.

"How many will be here for dinner? Your father will need to know," Teresa said.

Tom glanced towards Ellie and Lauren. Ellie nodded while Lauren shook her head. He looked up towards his mother again. "Only one extra."

Teresa nodded and then frowned. "It looks like you need a haircut, Sam. Do you want me to make an appointment for you next week?"

Sam blushed and shook his head. "I'm growing it."

Ellie wondered if that decision had anything to do with her comment on how he should wear his hair.

A man joined Teresa on the patio. His sandy brown hair was nearly as short as Tom's. He had sharp blue eyes and similar features to his oldest son, but his nose was hooked and his cheekbones more prominent. "Afternoon everyone."

Lauren grabbed Ellie's arm with a gasp. Ellie looked at her friend in surprise. Lauren continued to watch the patio.

"Dad, this is Beth and Lauren. My father, Gregory."

"Hi," Ellie said, nudging Lauren who still didn't reply.

"You've all got the right idea for a warm day like this," Gregory said.

"When doesn't Tom find some excuse to drag everyone into the pool?" Sam asked.

Gregory laughed. "I'll let you get back to your fun."

Chapter Fifteen

When Gregory and Teresa disappeared inside, Lauren shook Ellie's arm. "You didn't recognise him?"

Sam rolled his eyes. "Not you."

Tom laughed. "I bet Ellie doesn't have anything at all to do with cooking, other than eating the finished product."

Ellie looked from one to the other. "None of you are making sense."

"Gregory Wallace has his own cooking show," Lauren squealed.

"As in, on TV?" When Lauren nodded, Ellie asked, "What are you doing watching cooking shows?"

Lauren shook her head. "Sometimes you worry me." She pointed at Tom and Sam. "Their Dad is on TV."

"Guess that'd be why me asking if he's camera shy was amusing." Ellie met Tom's gaze.

Tom grinned. "Yep."

"Ellie!"

She turned to Lauren. "What?"

"He's famous." Lauren pointed towards the upper level of the house.

"He can't be too famous. I didn't recognise him," Ellie said.

"Hello? You wouldn't recognise an apron, you have so little to do with cooking. He has books out and everything."

Ellie tilted her head thoughtfully. "That makes sense."

Lauren frowned. "That he has books out?"

Ellie shook her head. "No. Why Sam can cook so well."

"It doesn't bother you Dad's on TV?" Sam asked.

"He cooks. How famous can he be? Lauren's mum watches every cooking and gardening show on TV. Even ones that might be on late at night because no one's interested in watching them." She nearly groaned at how much like an insult that sounded. "Ah... I didn't mean to insinuate no one watches your dad's show. So... uhm... are we going to get back in the pool? I'm getting cold standing around here talking." Ellie looked from Sam to Tom.

Tom grinned and jumped towards the pool, tucking his legs up. Ellie turned her head at the last second before the splash reached her. She quickly followed him. When he swam towards the shallow end, she swam after him, wondering what he was up to. He stopped and waited for her when the water was just over his shoulders. It was still a little deep for Ellie. She held onto Tom so she didn't have to tread water to keep her head above the surface.

"Have you never seen Dad on TV?" Tom wrapped his arms around her.

"I don't have any secret fantasy to be a brilliant chef. I have a terrible habit of setting kitchens on fire. Why would I bother watching cooking shows?"

Tom laughed. "Some people can't watch his shows enough."

"Who? Bored housewives and little old grannies?"

Tom continued to grin. "Yeah, something like that. Want to do another few laps?"

"No way. The only way I'm doing another lap of the pool is if someone either tows me or gives me a ride."

Tom's lips met Ellie's. "Sure I can't convince you?" He kissed her again.

"Nope. I'm going to laze on the steps and you can show me how fast you can swim. I know you can go faster than Sam and you can definitely swim faster than me."

"It won't bother you?"

Ellie grinned. "What won't bother me?"

"Me leaving you on your own while I do a few laps."

"Me lazing in the shallows so I can drool over your body as you swim back and forth?"

Tom kissed her again. "Need a ride to those shallows?"

"Yep." Ellie moved to Tom's back when he tapped it and held on. She took a deep breath when Tom slid beneath the water and watched as the end of the pool rapidly came closer.

A few minutes after Tom left her on the steps, Lauren joined her. Ellie grinned at her. "Did you get an autograph yet?"

"He's famous," Lauren insisted.

"Yep."

"Oh stop humouring me. You're completely uncultured."

"Because I don't watch cooking shows?"

Lauren giggled. "Okay. Fine. But he's still famous."

Ellie shrugged. "Now if he was in a band and

played lead guitar I might think about asking for his autograph, but a cook?" She shook her head. "I'll be right." She frowned. "Maybe I better stay away from him. What if setting kitchens on fire is contagious? Although it might make his shows more interesting."

Lauren hit Ellie lightly on the arm. "You're a lost cause."

"Yep."

"I've got to head soon. Are you set for the night?"

Ellie nodded. "Yeah. I'm here the entire weekend."

Lauren glanced towards Tom. "It looks like our planning didn't turn out too bad after all. I swear if you fell in an industrial bin you'd probably find a suitcase of money."

"As long as it wasn't a kitchen I fell into. Then it'd probably go up in flames."

Lauren giggled. "Hopeless."

"Yep. Absolutely."

They fell quiet as Sam swum over to them. He looked at Ellie. "You don't mind if I ride home with Lauren?"

"Not at all. But I'd suggest you pack a snack. She's always starved after a long ride."

Sam nodded. "I know. She asked for something to eat almost the moment she stepped inside this morning."

"Only because I'm madly in love with your cooking," Lauren said.

Sam blushed. "Do you want to use the bathroom first?"

Lauren shook her head. "Nah, you go ahead. I want to finish talking to Ellie."

Sam nodded and climbed out of the pool. Lauren watched him walk away. She sighed when he disappeared around the corner of the house.

"So what's your verdict?"

Lauren looked confused. "Huh?"

"The kiss?"

Lauren smiled slowly. "Not bad. Not bad at all."

"Do I take it there'll be more?"

"Maybe." Lauren's smile became a grin.

"Your mum's going to ground you for life before she let's a boy in the house."

"I've got the perfect plan."

"Then hurry up and tell me," Ellie said.

"Sam is getting a couple of signed pictures of his dad. She'll welcome him like a long lost son. She thinks Gregory Wallace is better than any lead guitar player."

Ellie rolled her eyes. "Only because she doesn't think a guitar is an instrument."

Lauren giggled. "Okay, better than anybody in any orchestra you could name."

"Well that wouldn't be hard since I couldn't name a single orchestra."

"Didn't I say you were uncultured?"

"I'll agree now. But cooking shows aren't culture."

"Okay. Fine. But my mum does love them."

Ellie looked thoughtful. "Did you decide Sam had potential before or after you learned who his father is?"

"Before."

Ellie nodded. "That's good. He's odd, but nice. Even though you're my best friend I wouldn't be able to sit back and let you use him."

"You aren't using Tom just for a place to stay on weekends?"

Ellie shook her head. "Nope. I'm only here because I can't keep my hands off him."

"That's nice to know."

Ellie and Lauren both turned to see that Tom had quietly surfaced not far from them. Lauren quickly stood up, hopping out of the pool. "I've got to go. Thanks for putting up with me." She was gone before either of them could say goodbye.

"I think I just embarrassed your friend." Tom sat on the step beside Ellie.

"Ah… yeah… I guess."

"And you?"

Ellie half smiled and shrugged. "Maybe. A little. We didn't hear you. How long were you listening?"

"Not long."

"Exactly how long?"

"From just before you were calling my brother odd again."

Ellie frowned as she tried to think back over what they'd said. She couldn't recall anything drastic. Her frown disappeared when Tom kissed her.

"There was nothing for you to be worried about. So what do you want to do now? We're about to have all of downstairs to ourselves."

Ellie grinned. "Behave."

"That doesn't sound like much fun."

Chapter Sixteen

Ellie sat quietly in the car beside Tom. The weekend had gone by too quickly. They pulled up in front of her house and Tom started to unbuckle his seat belt.

Ellie placed her hand over his. "Don't come in, Tom."

"More secrets?"

Ellie shook her head. "There's been a weekend long party. I don't want you to see that mess."

"Who cleans up after it?"

"I do."

Tom undid his seat belt.

"Tom–"

"I'll give you a hand."

Ellie sighed. She knew how stubborn Tom could be. Especially when he had that expression. "Fine. Don't complain. Remember I told you not to come in." She grabbed her schoolbag and overnight bag, that were at her feet, and got out of the car. She was just past the gate when Tom reached her side, taking her bags. Getting out her key, she unlocked the front door. As she let it swing open she watched Tom's face. His expression didn't change. She grinned. "You're good, I'll give you that much."

Tom dragged his gaze back to Ellie. "Good?"

"At neutral expressions."

Tom chuckled. "What were you expecting? That I'd run screaming to my car?"

Ellie shook her head. "Nah, you're too stubborn for that." She picked her way through the mess to her bedroom door. Unlocking it, she dumped her bags inside then closed the door again. Before she could move away from her door, Tom put his arms around her and pulled her close.

"Is this what you come home to every Sunday evening?"

"We're not having this discussion."

"One question only." Tom stared at her, waiting.

"Fine. One question. No more."

Tom nodded. "Is it?"

"Yeah."

Tom's lips brushed against hers. "Where do we start?"

Ellie grinned. "I hope that question was meant to be about cleaning up."

Tom laughed. "Yeah. I know exactly where I plan to start when it comes to-"

Ellie placed her fingers against his lips. "Don't get me distracted. It'll take hours to clean this mess up." She stepped out of Tom's arms and headed for the kitchen. She pulled out two garbage bags and handed one to Tom.

Ellie was surprised that Tom stuck around until the house was spotless, even helping her clean the bathroom. She put the last dish back in the kitchen cupboard before she turned to him. "Thanks."

Tom shrugged. "What do you plan to have for dinner? The place is empty again."

"I've got some packet soup in my bedroom."

"You've got to be kidding."

Ellie grinned. "And now you lose your neutral expression."

"What can I say? My father's a chef. We've been raised to think food is the meaning of life." He returned her grin.

"You won't get any arguments from me. Not about the food your family cooks. Well, your brother and father. I haven't tasted anything you've cooked yet."

"I rarely cook."

"Because?"

"There are people who like to do it more than I do."

"As good as it'll get around here is a cup of soup. You interested?"

"I'll put the kettle on if you get the soup." Tom filled the kettle at the sink.

Ellie grabbed the box of soup from her room and took it back to the kitchen. Tom had placed two mugs on the bench while she'd been gone. Opening the box, she took out two packets and tipped the contents into the mugs. Tom wrapped his arms around her, nuzzling her neck as they waited for the kettle to boil.

"How long have you been home?"

Ellie turned, Tom's arms falling away from her. "Couple of hours, I guess." She grabbed the Panadol off the top of the fridge, handing them to her mum. She was relieved to see her mum wore a dress rather than her ratty dressing gown and overly short nightie.

Sharon swallowed three and dropped the card of tablets onto the island bench. "Who are you?"

Tom stepped forward, holding out his hand. "Tom Wallace."

Sharon shook his hand. "You Ellie's boyfriend?"

"Ahh…" he glanced over to Ellie who grinned at his discomfort. He turned back to Sharon. "I guess."

"I didn't think it was that difficult a question. How did she meet you?"

"We go to the same school."

"I didn't know they had a special education unit there." Sharon spied the packet of soup. "Make me one, Ellie?"

Ellie took out another mug. "He's a swimmer, Mum. People that do sports aren't expected to do as well at school."

"I–" Tom began but stopped when both Ellie and Sharon burst out laughing. He shook his head instead. "So do I get a pass or a fail?"

Sharon shrugged. "It's only the first test. I don't start marking until they're all completed."

Tom nodded. "Fair enough."

Sharon took the mug Ellie handed her. "I don't mind this one, Ellie. He's actually got a sense of humour." She headed to the sofa and dropped onto it. "Turn the TV on will you, Ellie?"

Ellie handed Tom a mug and picked up the other mug before she headed over to turn on the television. "Leave your keycard out for me in the morning? I need to go shopping."

Sharon nodded. "Grab toilet paper too. We're down to the last roll."

Ellie nodded and then looked over to Tom. "Coming?" She headed to her room.

Tom glanced towards Sharon before he followed her. When Ellie closed and locked the door behind them, he said, "Should I ask why you're locking us in?"

Ellie grinned. "Because Mum is likely to come bursting in here in the hope of embarrassing you."

"Do you always go shopping Monday afternoon?"

Ellie nodded, then took a sip of her soup. "Yeah. I only get a week's worth of groceries."

"How do you normally get it home?"

"Walk."

"You carry it all at once?"

Ellie shook her head. "What do I look like? Superwoman? I do several trips."

"Do you want a lift?"

"Only if you're not doing anything else. I've been taking care of myself for years, Tom."

He put his mug on the duchess and placed hers next to his. "I know." He wrapped his arms around her. "I'm not asking if you need my help, I'm asking if you mind me tagging along with you."

"Oh you're good. What are you planning to be? A diplomat?"

Tom shook his head. "Nah, I'll leave that to my mother. I'm planning on doing a Bachelor of Exercise Science/Bachelor of Business focused on sport management."

"That's a mouthful. How long will that take you to finish?"

"Four years."

"That's not too bad. Have you figured out which uni and what grades you need?"

Tom nodded. "How did we get onto this conversation?"

Ellie laughed. "It happens. What I want to know about is your comment about your mother and being a diplomat."

"She's currently on leave or whatever they call it. But she's worked for the Department of Foreign Affairs and Trade for a long time. When we were younger we stayed in a couple of different countries. She's currently deciding if she wants to continue with the work. Now that Dad's career has taken off, he'd like to stay in Australia for a while."

"I didn't know diplomats still existed. I thought it was a job that ceased to exist decades ago. I was only joking when I asked if you were going to be one.

"Nah, they're not extinct yet." Tom yawned.

Ellie rested her head against his shoulder. "I guess you should go home soon."

"I could probably be convinced to stay a little longer."

Ellie laughed, looking up at him. "I bet you could."

Tom grinned. "I take it that's a no?"

Ellie kissed him. "Are you giving me a lift to school tomorrow?"

Tom nodded. "Yeah. Why?"

"Can I please sleep in? Pick me up at quarter past?"

"That'll only give you another fifteen minutes."

"Please?"

"Okay." Tom kissed her and the conversation ended temporarily. He drew back reluctantly. "Still no?"

Ellie smiled. "Still no." She moved away to unlock the door, walking out to the car with him. Sharon was no longer in the lounge room.

Tom leaned against his car, his arms wrapped loosely around her waist. "What've you got for breakfast tomorrow? More soup?"

"Breakfast bar. Stop worrying about me. I've been–"

Tom interrupted. "I know, taking care of yourself for years." He kissed her before she could comment.

"I'll see you tomorrow." He let her go, turned her and gently pushed her towards the house before he got into his car.

Striding to the house, Ellie stopped when she reached the doorway, turning to watch Tom drive away. Smiling, she locked the door and got ready for bed.

* * *

Ellie glared at Tom and Sam as she put a packet of soup in the trolley. "Haven't you two got anything better to talk about other than the contents of my trolley?"

Tom and Sam shared a look before Tom answered with a grin. "Nope."

Ellie rolled her eyes, stalking down the aisle. She weighed up walking home with her groceries against Tom and Sam criticising her eating habits. She sighed. Okay, so she was stuck with them. She hurried through the rest of the shopping and headed for a checkout. Her hands hovered over the flour she hadn't put in the trolley. Then she spied a bottle of vanilla essence and cocoa. She knew who was to blame.

Sam shrugged when her gaze landed on him.

"You're nearly out of flour and you need the other stuff."

Ellie shook her head and started to put the groceries on the conveyor belt. She found several more items as she went. At least they were all food that was kept in a cupboard. She'd be able to keep them in her bedroom so they weren't used on the weekend. Except the flour. No one was ever interested in flour.

When they arrived home, Tom and Sam helped her put the groceries away. Neither of them commented when she put the extra items Sam had thrown in the trolley in her room.

When everything was away, Sam looked from Ellie to Tom. "How long are you staying?"

"Ellie?"

She shrugged when Tom turned to her. "I don't have anything planned." She faced Sam. "Why?"

"I was thinking of walking over to see Lauren. It's only ten minutes from here."

Ellie smiled. Sam had joined her and Lauren at lunchtime, bringing with him custard Danishes. It had been odd having another person hanging out with them all lunch, but before the bell rang Sam had actually managed to talk to Lauren without any awkwardness. Tom had joined them until his friends had dragged him away to play some sport involving a ball. She just couldn't remember which game it had been.

"Are you going to stick around for a bit?" Ellie stepped closer to Tom.

He nodded. His gaze didn't leave Ellie as he spoke to Sam. "I'll give you a call when I'm leaving and pick you up on the way."

Ellie tugged Tom towards her room, kicking the door shut behind them. They tumbled onto her bed, jolted back to their surroundings nearly an hour later when Ellie's mobile phone rang. She hesitated. Her lips clung to Tom's a moment longer before she grabbed her phone from the floor, sitting up to answer it.

She listened as the person on the other end identified themselves as being from the hospital. A sense of unreality washed over her as they continued to speak. Once the conversation was over, she carefully placed her phone on the chest of drawers beside the bed, staring down at it.

Chapter Seventeen

"Are you okay?" Tom asked. "That was a really quick conversation."

Ellie nodded, continuing to stare at her phone. Her mind tried to process the call. It was impossible.

"Ellie?"

"Can you give me a lift to the hospital?"

"What?"

"My mum was in some sort of an accident. It didn't make a lot of sense." Ellie frowned. "A park, a long flight of concrete steps and a skateboarder knocking her down them. Can you give me a lift?"

"Of course I can." Tom was instantly on his feet, straightening his clothes.

Ellie continued to sit on the bed. She looked up when Tom held out his hand in front of her. He waited patiently. She stared at him a moment longer before she took his hand and let him pull her to her feet. She looked around, trying to figure out what she needed. Her fingers wrapped around her phone as she picked up her small handbag.

The trip to the hospital was a blur. She remembered telling Tom to pick her up in an hour and a half, but that was about it. She didn't think there'd been any other conversation, but she couldn't be absolutely certain. She asked the woman at the desk where her mum was and was soon standing by her bed. Sharon looked terrible. Plaster, bruises, scrapes and a drip in her arm.

"Mum." Ellie's word was part whisper, part exclamation and part plea. On the heels of the worry over her mum came worry for herself. There was no way she could live with her father if anything happened to Sharon. Pamela probably wouldn't allow it anyway.

Sharon blinked several times, her eyes only half open. "Ellie? What're you doing here? How'd they track you down?" Her words were slurred.

"I put my phone number in your phone under ICE."

"Never noticed it." Sharon's eyes drifted closed.

"What happened, Mum?"

"Stupid little bastard on a skateboard. Came out of nowhere. Didn't have time to get out of his way. I was taking a shortcut through a park. That flight of stairs that cuts through the hill is easier than walking around the block, but now it's full of skateboarders. Your boyfriend doesn't skate, does he?"

Ellie shrugged. "I don't know. Not as far as I've noticed."

Before Sharon could say anything else, there was a knock on the door. Sharon and Ellie's gazes were drawn to the doorway as they waited for whoever had knocked to enter. Ellie didn't recognise the woman. Although she did remind her of Pamela, with her high heels, painted nails and pale hair drawn back from her face.

"Are you Elizabeth Malloy?"

Ellie nodded. Her mum had rarely ever agreed with anything her father had suggested. Every time she heard her first name it made her wonder why her mum had gone along with the name. Her paternal grandmother had never been interested in meeting her, why would she want to be named after her?

"Could I talk to you for a few minutes? Maybe out in the corridor?"

Ellie shook her head. "What's wrong with here?" She didn't have a good feeling about this.

The woman glanced to where her mum lay in the bed.

Sharon scowled at the woman. "Just get on with it. I'm not about to leave my girl alone with you."

The woman hesitated again. "I'm from the Department of Child Safety. I understand it's just you and your mother at home. The hospital notified me."

Ellie looked at Sharon who shrugged and then winced. She turned back to the woman, her sense of dread increasing. "What's the problem?"

"Your mother will be in hospital for a minimum of two weeks. We need to make arrangements for somewhere for you to stay."

"What sort of arrangements?" Ellie asked cautiously.

"If you have no other family you can stay with, we can arrange for you to temporarily go into foster care."

When Ellie saw her mum's expression, she shook her head, trying to keep her own expression neutral. "I'm fine, thanks." They both had bad memories of that time.

The woman looked surprised. "Where will you be staying?"

"With my father. He won't mind. He always complains he doesn't see enough of me." Ellie noticed her mum relaxed at her words.

"Could I have his number so we can confirm this?"

"Do you have a business card? I'd have to ring you back with the number. I'm hopeless at remembering numbers off by heart." But really good at making up stories on the spot. Ellie smiled innocently and took the card when the woman handed it to her. She looked at the name. "Heather. Is that you?" When the woman nodded, Ellie tucked the card into her pocket. "I'll give you a call tomorrow then."

Heather looked like she wanted to say something else. Instead, she nodded. "I'll talk to you then." Her gaze shifted to Sharon. "I wish you a speedy recovery." She hurried out of the room, leaving silence in her wake.

"You going to stay with him?" Sharon finally asked.

"Preferably not. I'll be okay."

Sharon smiled slightly and then winced. "Stupid bitch. You can probably take care of yourself better than she takes care of herself."

"Don't worry about it, Mum. I'm not. I'm going to head now. I've got school tomorrow. Is there anything I can bring you when I visit you tomorrow afternoon?"

"Yeah. They won't give me a drink. Tried to tell me I've got a problem. What the hell would they know?"

"Okay. Don't worry about it. I'll bring you something tomorrow."

Sharon reached out to Ellie who stepped forward to take her hand. "You're a good kid. Better than a clone kid like Stupid Bitch has."

Ellie smiled. She guessed her mum wasn't feeling too bad if she was running Pamela down and asking for a drink. Everything seemed almost normal. "I'll see you tomorrow." She bent forward and carefully placed a kiss on Sharon's cheek between a scrape and a bruise.

"Don't forget what I asked for," Sharon called out as Ellie reached the doorway.

Ellie turned back. "Of course I won't."

When Ellie was out the front of the hospital, she glanced at the time on her phone. Tom was due to pick her up in about twenty minutes. She was surprised at how little time had passed. She'd thought it would take longer. Finding a seat to sit on, she waited. Tom was ten minutes early and nodded his head when Ellie said she didn't want to talk about it yet. On the way home, Ellie had Tom pull up at a pub Sharon regularly frequented.

It didn't take her long to convince one of her mum's friends to buy two medium sized bottles of scotch. She withdrew money from the ATM that sat in one corner. When she hopped back in the car, Tom remained silent. He reached for her hand as soon as he pulled up in front of her house.

"You'll let me know if there's anything I can do?"

Ellie nodded.

"Is your mum going to be all right?"

Ellie nodded again. At least that was what she'd been told.

"Do you still want me to pick you up in the morning?"

Ellie nodded.

"Are you ever going to speak again?"

Ellie smiled and threw her arms around Tom. "Thank you." She hopped out of the car and hurried to the front door. Tom drove off the moment she stepped inside. The house seemed quiet so she turned on the television. About half an hour later, there was a knock on the door.

Ellie wished she hadn't turned on the television so she could have pretended she wasn't home. The last thing she wanted to do was talk to anyone. She didn't feel in the least bit sociable. There was another knock on the door.

"Elizabeth? Are you okay in there?"

Ellie nearly cringed when she heard Heather's voice. She pulled out her phone and sent a text to

Tom. *Please pick me up. ASAP.* What was Heather doing here? How did she get her address?

"Yeah. I'm just packing my bag. I can't turn up on my father's doorstep without any clothes." Ellie looked at her phone when it beeped. *Still at Lauren's. Five minutes away.* She breathed a sigh of relief. "I can't stop to talk. My ride will be here in a few minutes." She hurried to her room and threw some clothes in her overnight bag.

"Your father is happy for you to stay with him?" Heather called out.

Ellie grabbed her schoolbag, shoved the alcohol into her overnight bag and headed back to the lounge room where she turned off the television. Unlocking the door, she stepped onto the verandah. Leaving the verandah light on, she locked the door and started to walk away, still wondering what Heather was doing at her home.

"Aren't you going to turn off the light?" Heather pointed upwards.

Pausing on the edge of the verandah, Ellie shook her head. "We leave it on permanently. Day and night. Habit I guess. Probably a bad one."

"How did your father take the news you'd be staying with him for a while?" Heather asked.

Ellie saw Tom's car pull up in front of her house

and felt like cheering. "That's my ride. I better go. I'll call you tomorrow." She dashed to the car before Heather could say anything else. "Get out of here in a hurry," Ellie said the moment she shut the car door. She noticed Sam was in the back.

Tom pulled away from the curb. "What's going on?"

"I'm meant to be staying at my father's since my mum's in hospital. I don't know why the hospital had to interfere. Why can't they mind their own business?"

"Does that mean you're asking if you can crash at my place tonight?" Tom asked.

"Yeah. Do you mind?"

Tom shook his head. "Nah, it's fine. Who was on your verandah?"

"Some woman who wants to put me in a foster home."

"What?" Tom and Sam exclaimed together.

"They don't want me to stay home alone. I guess they're worried something might happen to me. It's not like I'm a little kid."

"Do you think if you talked it over with them they'd let you stay at your home? Explain you don't need a babysitter or something," Sam asked.

"I wasn't going to stick around long enough for

her to give me a definite no. It's okay. I'll just pretend we're at war and it's… what did they call it decades ago… dark or something. You know, when they were being bombed. That way no one will know I'm at home."

"Blackout. They reduced the amount of lights in towns and cities to make it harder for enemy aircraft to find targets of a night. They even tarred the windows in some buildings," Sam said.

Ellie grinned. "Yeah, something like that."

"Night vision goggles made the tactic obsolete," Sam said.

"All right. Now we're getting to the 'too much info' point."

"Sorry," Sam muttered.

Ellie turned in her seat so she could see Sam. "That's okay. So, how was your afternoon with Lauren?" She laughed when Sam blushed. "That good, huh?"

Tom rested his hand on her thigh. "Stop teasing my brother."

Ellie grinned. "Spoil sport. It doesn't matter anyway. I'll ask Lauren later. She'll tell me." She laughed at the odd sound that came from the back seat. Her laughter dried up when Tom's hand began to make lazy movements. She looked over at him and their gazes clashed for a second before his attention returned to the road.

She'd have to say one thing for Heather. Turning up on her doorstep like that had made her stop worrying about her mum for a bit.

Chapter Eighteen

Ellie didn't have time to talk to Lauren until lunch the next day. She couldn't ask her about her afternoon with Sam since he joined them, with his offering of food. She also didn't have time to ask her in the afternoon as Tom gave her a lift to the hospital.

She wriggled into cargo pants, slipping her skirt off. "Keep your eyes on the road," she muttered when Tom glanced her way again.

"Then stop doing a striptease beside me," Tom said.

She pulled a baggy shirt on over her school shirt and sat up straighter so she could do up her cargo pants. Glancing in the back, she was relieved to see that Sam still stared out the side window. "All dressed." She slipped the two medium sized bottles of scotch into the pockets of her pants and slung her bag over her shoulder, ready to get out the moment they reached the hospital. "What's that look mean?" Ellie stared at Tom.

He shook his head. "Ask me again later if you really want to know."

"Fine," Ellie muttered as she unbuckled. "An hour?" When Tom nodded, she leaned forward, kissed him and got out of the car. She watched as he drove off.

Ellie headed to her mum's room, not needing to ask directions this time. She paused in the doorway. The colours of the bruising looked even more spectacular today. Sharon's eyes opened and she tried to smile when she saw Ellie. She winced. Her swollen lips had several cuts on them. Ellie walked into the room to stand beside her mum.

"I won't ask how you're feeling. You look dreadful." Ellie glanced around before she pulled one of the bottles out. She cracked the seal then handed it to her mum.

"I won't be writing you out of the will now." Sharon took a large drink. "They're trying to kill me in here." She eyed the bottle. "Is this all you brought?"

Ellie shook her head and pulled out the other bottle. She broke the seal, tightened the lid and slid it under the blankets. "You didn't get them from me." She grinned.

"That woman was here again today."

"Who?"

"The one from last night who thought you were a little kid."

"Ahh, Heather. Yeah, she was bugging me at home too."

"Said she hadn't heard from you. She tracked down your father and he rang me wanting to know what was going on. I told them we decided school was too important for you to ditch a couple of weeks of it. You've only got a bit over a month left. Bloody idiots."

"Thanks, Mum. What else did you tell her?"

"Told her I was too exhausted to talk. Pressed the buzzer for a nurse and they threw her out."

Ellie grinned. "Nice."

"That's what I thought. Interfering bitch. And your father wouldn't stop nagging either. So what's the plan, Ellie?"

"Good question. I'm working on that." She glanced at the time. "I'll have to leave in about twenty minutes."

"You be back tomorrow? These bottles will be well and truly empty by then." Sharon slid the one she held under the blanket. "Red alert," Sharon whispered, her gaze sliding past Ellie.

Ellie turned and nearly groaned when she saw

Heather standing in the doorway. She turned back to her mum and winked. "It won't take me long to get that for you Mum. I'll run and you'll barely notice me gone."

Sharon nodded. "Well don't take too long." She looked towards Heather. "Come in then. You might as well, rather than clutter up the doorway."

"I need to talk to you, Elizabeth," Heather said when Ellie tried to walk past her.

"I'll be back in a few minutes. Try not to wear Mum out while I'm gone."

"Like you rang me today with your father's phone number?" Heather continued to stand in the doorway.

Ellie shrugged. "It didn't seem much point when I had a change of plans. Why would you need me to ring you with his number when I wasn't going to stay there after all?"

"And yet when I rang him, he didn't have a clue you were going to stay with him."

"Of course not. He's my dad, isn't he? I should be able to rock up whenever I like. And a good thing I didn't ring him and bother him when we figured out it'd be better to stick around here. Can we finish this conversation when I get back?"

Heather continued to stand in the doorway.

"Where are you staying now? Your father is extremely concerned and his wife said you really shouldn't be left at home alone. That you aren't even capable of preparing a simple meal without setting the kitchen on fire."

She really, really hated Pamela. "I'm staying with friends."

"Your mother didn't seem to know where you were staying."

Ellie turned to her mum. "I wasn't sure if you were properly awake when I told you. Guess you weren't. I'm staying with Sam. You remember Sam, don't you, Mum? The super geeky one."

"Of course," Sharon said, even though she hadn't met him.

Ellie faced Heather again. "There you go, all sorted. No problems at all."

"Is Sam your boyfriend?"

Ellie laughed. "No way. You have to be joking."

"How can I be joking or otherwise when I wouldn't have a clue what the situation is? What is Sam's phone number?"

"Ellie, have you forgotten you're meant to be running an errand for me? It's not like I can get out of this bed and do things for myself. Really, some people are so inconsiderate." Sharon glared at Heather.

"Yep. Sorry, Mum." Ellie pushed past Heather and dashed for the stairs. She didn't want to wait for the elevator and risk Heather catching up with her. She didn't think the woman would be able to run very fast in the high heels she wore, but just in case, she didn't slow down until she was on the ground floor. A glance around showed her the way was still clear and she headed outside to wait for Tom, breathing a sigh of relief when she saw he waited for her.

"What's up with you?" Tom asked when he started the car.

"I swear I'm going to start getting more exercise. I'm so unfit." She buckled up and looked in the mirror. "God! Could I be any redder in the face?" She glanced in the back seat. "Hey, where's Sam?"

"Home. Where do you want to go?"

"I guess I should go home. Oh, and before I forget, what was it you wouldn't discuss with me earlier?"

Tom was silent a few minutes before he spoke. "Should you be taking alcohol up to your mother? It might give her a chance to dry out."

"Don't start on me."

"I just thought-"

"You don't know anything about it. I want her to stay in hospital and get better. Not try and drag herself home so she can drink herself senseless. If I take her up some alcohol every day that'll help keep her in there. Until she's willing to admit she has a problem no one can help her because she doesn't believe she needs help."

"You shouldn't have to deal with this, Ellie."

"It's my choice. I could have let my father put me in a boarding school and forgot all about Mum. At least if I stay I not only get to run my own life, but I can make sure there's food for her when she's hungry, her bills are paid and she has a clean house to live in."

"It's not your responsibility."

"Whose responsibility is it?"

"Hers."

Ellie shook her head. "If someone was disabled would you say it was their fault?" Tom parked the car in front of Ellie's house. "Drive along two houses."

He moved the car without questioning her. "That's completely different."

"No. It isn't. Alcoholism is a sickness. She can't help it. And until she figures out there's a problem, we can't help her either. She'd just kick me out of her life like she did Dad. And then where would she be?"

"Can I come in?"

Ellie stared at Tom for a couple of minutes before she shook her head. "Best not to."

"Is it because of what I said about the alcohol?"

"No." She smiled wryly. "I might not let you go home once I get you inside."

"Do you want me to stay?"

Ellie laughed. "Definitely not a good idea. The two of us alone, in the dark."

"That doesn't exactly bother you when you're at my place."

"We're not alone. Your parents are upstairs and your brother is in the room next door. Are you picking me up tomorrow morning?"

"Yeah." Tom leaned close and kissed her.

Ellie reluctantly pulled away. "See you in the morning." She glanced around to make sure Heather was nowhere in sight before she hopped out of the car.

As soon as she was inside, Ellie quickly made something to eat and drew all the curtains. Before it was completely dark she showered and hung a heavy blanket across her window so she could have her laptop on without the light showing outside. Plugging her headphones into the laptop, she put them on. Next she checked her emails and had to smother her laughter when she clicked on the link one of her friends had sent her of a swearing cockatoo on Youtube. Then she signed into her messenger. She was barely signed in when she had six windows pop up all at once wanting to talk to her. She typed brb in all the windows, except for the one that would be the quickest to chat to, and set her status as busy. She quickly talked to and said goodbye to most of them.

Ellie says: Hey.

Society of Australian Magicians says: How are you?

Ellie says: Okay.

Society of Australian Magicians says: Was just checking. Lauren said a really big chocolate cake would cheer you up.

Ellie says: lol. And I bet she's expecting me to share it with her.

Society of Australian Magicians says: Probably : D

Ellie says: I wouldn't turn it down ;)

Society of Australian Magicians says: Done.

Ellie says: Really?

Society of Australian Magicians says: Yeah.

Ellie says: Thanks. You're brilliant : D

Ellie says: I've g2g. Still have your brother and Lauren waiting to talk to me. I get confused if I have too many conversations going at once. End up typing in the wrong window *goes red with embarrassment*

Society of Australian Magicians says: lol.

Ellie says: Buh-bye.

Society of Australian Magicians says: Night.

TW says: What is taking you so long to answer? Longest brb I've ever experienced.

Ellie says: Give me a chance. I'm a wanted woman : D

TW says: Now that I'd believe. I'm sure I've seen a poster of you in a police station.

Ellie says: Very funny.

TW says: : D

Ellie says: Lauren's waiting to talk to me.

TW says: I'm waiting to talk to you.

Ellie says: I'm worth the wait, aren't I?

TW says: Hmmm.

Ellie says: Think carefully how you answer now-Lisbeth.

TW says: Hurry up and finish talking to Lauren.

Ellie says: Will do.

Ellie says: Back.

Miaow is cat for PLEASE says: Finally *rolls eyes* what took you so long?

Ellie says: Haven't been online a lot lately. Everyone wanted to know if I was still alive.

Miaow is cat for PLEASE says: I've g2g to bed in about ten. I have so much to tell you and ask you.

Ellie says: brb. Sorry. Just knocked a cup off my

desk. Better check to see if it's in one piece. At least I'd finished drinking it.

Miaow is cat for **PLEASE** says: Hurry.

Ellie stubbed her toe as she got up from the desk and the chair nearly hit the floor. She caught it, but kicked the cup across the floor. Opening her mouth to swear, she froze when she heard a knock on the front door. She fought the urge to check out the window and held her breath. Another knock.

"I know someone is in there. I heard a noise," Heather called out.

Ellie carefully sat back at her laptop and sent the same message to both Lauren and Tom.

Ellie says: Very important you don't send another message until I tell you it's all clear. Don't even acknowledge this message.

Chapter Nineteen

Ellie set her status as offline and returned to the page she still had up of the swearing cockatoo.

"Hello? Elizabeth? Are you in there?"

Ellie unplugged the headphones and pressed play. She smiled as she listened to the cockatoo squawk. She made note of the time on the bar and took it back to there once it was finished. She paused it. Heather was silent outside. She played the squawking section again. Still quiet.

Was she gone or did she wait to see if Ellie would give herself away. She didn't know. She plugged the headphones back in.

Ellie says: There's a woman out the front of my house that wants to put me in a foster home. I'm trying to pretend I'm not here.

Miaow is cat for PLEASE says: Your life is never dull!

Ellie says: I want dull : (

Miaow is cat for PLEASE says: lol. I've g2g now. That woman has ruined my night too. Had so much to tell you. And it's not like I can talk about Sam in front of him : D

Ellie says: Tell me one thing then.

Miaow is cat for PLEASE says: He turns seventeen in January! Won't have to hassle his brother for a lift then and his parents will buy him a car.

Ellie says: Nice.

Miaow is cat for PLEASE says: Yep. But have to go now. Catch you at school tomorrow. And hop online earlier tomorrow night. Pleeeaaase.

Ellie says: Will do. Buh-bye.

Miaow is cat for PLEASE says: Bibi.

Ellie unplugged the headphones and played the cockatoo squawking. Just in case. She hadn't heard any more knocks at the door, but that didn't mean Heather wasn't out there. Whatever happened to people working from nine to five? She didn't think she knew a single person who did. She plugged the headphones back in and was about to slip them on when she heard a phone ringing. It wasn't hers, but it reminded her to set hers to silent.

"I know I'm late."

Ellie grinned when she heard the annoyance in Heather's voice.

"Look, I'll be there in about an hour. Surely you can wait that long."

Ellie wished she could hear the other end of the conversation.

"This one is different. I know I can't save every kid, but I'm also not going to sit back and let another one die either. There's not enough funding to catch each one before they slip through the cracks."

Ellie glared at the covered window, wishing she could tell Heather that she was fine. That there was no need to worry about her.

"I can't expect you to understand. You haven't read all the reports I've read. You haven't talked to her father and stepmother. Kids don't always know that they don't have to accept the situation they're in. They feel obligated to stay. This kid can't even cook for herself. I spoke to one of her teachers after talking to her father and she confirmed it."

Ellie was torn between anger and amusement. Heather should mind her own business. So should her old Home Economics teacher. It had been years since the woman had been forced to teach her. You'd think she'd be over her near nervous breakdown by now.

"I don't need to talk to anyone. There's nothing wrong with me. It's these kids that need help. If I'd only put in more hours, not thought things could be left until I had more time, then he'd still be alive. So don't try and tell me that sixteen is old enough to look after yourself. He was a month off sixteen and that didn't help him at all."

Ellie rested her head in her hands. Great! She was stuck with some guilt ridden crusader. Why couldn't she have got someone who wasn't interested? She was fine. The only problem she currently had was Heather.

"Look, I have to go. I promised this one's father that I'd ring him back and let him know she was okay. Maybe I can convince him to come and see her."

Grinning, Ellie listened to the retreating footsteps. Heather would be a miracle worker if she could manage that. She slipped her headphones back on.

Ellie says: Sorry I took so long.

TW says: What's going on? I've been sitting here worried.

Ellie says: Heather, the one who wants to put me

in a foster home, was banging on my door. I accidentally made a noise just before she knocked. Had a swearing cockatoo that I'd been listening to. Someone sent me the link to it on Youtube. I'll send it to you. I played that to make her think it was only an animal she heard.

TW says: Nice save. She fall for it?

Ellie says: I don't know. I guess.

TW says: lol.

Ellie says: I wish she'd just leave me alone.

TW says: Why not stay at your father's for the couple of weeks your mum will be in hospital?

Ellie says: How much attention have you been paying to what goes on in my life?

TW says: Surely he'd take you in an emergency.

Ellie says: Do you still believe in Santa and the Easter bunny too?

TW says: Ha ha.

Ellie says: 1st problem- will miss out on too much school.

Ellie says: 2nd problem- he'd jump at the foster home option.

TW says: Would that be so bad?

Ellie says: YES! I've heard of kids going in temporarily and being a foster kid until they were old enough to leave home.

TW says: That wouldn't always happen. Besides, I've met foster kids that liked their foster home. And you're sixteen, leaving home wouldn't be that long away.

Ellie says: Not if Heather had anything to say about it. She thinks I'm completely incompetent so I'm not risking it. Can we drop the subject?

TW says: Do you have a list of subjects I'm allowed to discuss?

TW says: You still there? I'm sorry. Forget my last comment. Please.

Ellie says: Only if you do some heavy duty grovelling tomorrow.

TW says: Do I get to use my own style of grovelling?

Ellie says: Hmm. Maybe.

TW says: I promise you'll enjoy it : D

Ellie says: Deal.

* * *

Ellie yawned as she walked along the corridor to her mum's hospital room. It had been nearly one before she'd finished chatting to Tom. She wondered if he felt as tired as she did. Although he probably felt worse since he'd been up hours before her so he could go to the pool. After a long and boring day at school she wanted to curl up somewhere and sleep. Instead she was stuck making a delivery to her mum. She turned a corner and then quickly jumped back, pressing herself against the wall.

Heather was standing near her mum's door. At least Heather faced the other direction and hadn't seen her. She swore under her breath, wondering what to do. No way could she go another round with Heather. It was like trying to run through a field full of landmines. She sent a text to Tom. *Need help. Guard at the door. Need you to make the delivery.*

She headed back to the ground floor as she waited for Tom to reply. *Back in five.* She grinned when she read his text. She was beginning to think he could always be counted on. Which was a nice change. When she stepped outside he waited for her in his car. She hopped in and told him about Heather while he found a park in the multistorey car park.

Tom shook his head as he put the bottles of alcohol in his schoolbag. "Why do I suddenly feel like I'm in a movie about prohibition?"

Ellie grinned. "Make sure you get that moonshine through. No stopping for anything."

"I think this will cancel out the grovelling I was meant to do."

Ellie pouted. "But I was looking forward to it. You sure you don't want to show me, as a teaching exercise? Just in case I need the skill sometime in the future?"

Tom reached out and, with his hand at the back of her head, pulled her close to him. His lips met hers, deepening the kiss before he ended it. "Wait here for me."

Ellie nodded. She wasn't going anywhere near the hospital while Heather was prowling around inside. She wasn't crazy. Well, not that crazy anyway. She looked out the window and watched cars slowly drive past as they searched for a spot to park. Pulling out her phone, she checked the time. Then she tried to get more comfortable.

A sigh escaped and she now wished Sam hadn't wanted to be dropped home. Sitting by herself was boring her senseless. She checked the time again. Why did it move so slowly when you wanted it to go fast? Another car crept along, the backseat filled with blue balloons. Her foot tapped impatiently and she looked at the ignition. He had the keys with him. She should have asked him to leave the stereo on.

Anything would have been better than being left alone with her thoughts. She kept thinking back to when she was five-years-old and two strangers had entered their house, taking her away. Her father had been away at a conference and a busybody neighbour had rung the police because she was still playing outside late at night, with no supervision. It had taken her father two months to sort everything out and she hadn't seen her family once in all that time. She never ever wanted to go through that again.

Sleeping in a stranger's house, not knowing what to expect. Worrying about her mum. That had been the hardest part. Not knowing if her mum was okay. Knowing that there'd be no one there to look after her and worried she'd never see her again.

By the time Tom returned to the car, Ellie had been about to go and look for him. "What took you so long?"

Tom slid into the driver's seat and pulled the door shut. "Pounce on me why don't you?" He slung his bag onto the backseat.

"Don't keep me in suspense."

Tom started the car and reversed out. "Good thing you warned me about the cockatoo. She was trying to grill your mum about pets. I said you were looking after a friend's cockatoo while they were away on a camp."

"Good save."

"Your lies must be contagious."

"Yeah right. I bet you tell them better than me. Did you give Mum her bottles?"

"That's what took me so long. I had to play twenty questions with Heather before she'd leave. I wasn't going to make the delivery while she was watching."

"What did she ask you?"

"Did I know you? Had I seen you? Did I know where you were staying or how she could get in touch with you?" Tom shook his head. "That woman fired questions faster than Sam kills the enemy on his games."

"Thanks for doing that for me."

"Your mum said she's finally ready to grade my tests but she's not telling me the results."

Ellie grinned. "That means she likes you."

"Or she doesn't want to chase away the delivery boy.

Ellie laughed. "Nope. She likes you."

"So where am I taking you now?"

"Home."

"Sure you don't want to go somewhere."

Ellie hesitated, then shook her head. "Nah. I've got an assignment due on Friday and I haven't even started it."

"Need any help?"

"Do you think I'd get much work done?"

Tom grinned. "Maybe."

Ellie snorted. "Yeah, right. Not a single chance."

Chapter Twenty

Friday night Ellie huddled at the head of her bed, her arms wrapped around her legs that were drawn up so her chin rested on her knees. She flinched when there was more pounding on the front door.

"Come on, Sharon. Come out! Where are you, babe?" The shouted words were slurred and accompanied by echoes from other people.

"Sharon!"

"Where you at, girl?"

"Are we playing hide and seek?"

There was the sound of glass smashing and someone swore. "Sharon!"

Ellie rocked back and forth as she tried to block out the sounds. She'd been listening to people turning up since six. With each hour that passed they seemed to be getting drunker. Some of them were the same people, but mostly it was different ones. She'd thought about pinning a note on the door to say parties were cancelled till next year due to a hospital stay, but each time she'd thought it was safe, someone else had turned up. It was now half past ten and the flow of people seemed to be increasing rather than dropping off like she'd hoped.

Her mobile phone beeped and she reached out to check who had sent her a message. It was from Tom. *Where are you? I've been online for ages.*

Ellie closed her eyes. She'd forgotten her promise to chat with him online at eight. He was supposed to be getting an early night as he had a swim meet tomorrow. She forced herself to move over to the laptop and turn it on. She jumped when there was a bang against the front door. It sounded like something had been thrown against it. It was probably a good thing the neighbours were accustomed to noisy parties every weekend. Otherwise they might have called the police and Heather didn't need any more ammunition in her campaign to take over her life.

Ellie pulled her legs up under herself as she sat in front of the laptop. As soon as she was online she signed into her messenger as offline. She clicked on Tom's name.

Ellie says: Sorry.

TW says: What's up?

Ellie says: Nothing. Didn't mean to forget.

TW says: Why do I feel like you're lying to me?

Ellie says: Do you think I deliberately forgot?

TW says: No. And you know perfectly well what I meant. Should I come over there?

Ellie says: No.

TW says: Because…

Ellie says: You need to get some sleep.

TW says: How can I sleep if I'm worried about you?

Ellie says: There's nothing to worry about.

TW says: Liar.

Ellie says: Did you poke your tongue out when you said that?

Ellie's phone rang and she quickly picked it up. She frowned when she saw it was Tom. She sighed when she looked at her laptop screen.

TW says: Answer the phone!

TW says: What are you trying to hide?

She didn't have much choice other than to answer. "What?" She kept her voice low, but would have been surprised if anyone heard her with the amount of noise they were making outside.

"What the hell is going on in the background? Are you having a party there?"

"Not likely. I'd planned to have an early night. Someone's been keeping me up every night this week chatting online. Pretty sad when all I want to do on a Friday night is sleep."

"What's going on, Ellie?"

She sighed. She couldn't blame the television considering he knew she was aiming for total silence and no lights visible. She was just glad Heather had stopped trying to catch her at home.

"Ellie?"

"Mum's drinking mates have been turning up all evening looking for the party that's normally here." She jumped when there was another crash at the front door.

"What was that?"

"Hopefully not a battering ram."

"That's it, I'm coming to get you."

"No. I'm fine. Honest. Come on, Tom, you've got to get an early start tomorrow."

"Pack a bag. You're staying the weekend." He hung up.

Ellie swore and turned to her laptop.

Ellie says: Don't you dare come over here.

TW says: Not listening.

Ellie says: I'm not packing.

TW says: Then I'll drag you out of there in what you're wearing and you can live in it all weekend.

Ellie says: TOM!

TW says: Do you think I'm going to be able to sleep knowing you're putting up with that racket? What happens if they break the door down?

Ellie says: I'm locked in my room.

TW says: Too bad. I'll be there ASAP.

Ellie says: Please Tom. I'm fine.

TW says: I'll knock on your front door until you answer it.

Ellie says: Tom!

She glared at her screen when he logged out. Closing her laptop down, she put it in her overnight bag. Next she grabbed a handful of clothes, stuffed them in, slung her handbag over her shoulder and grabbed her schoolbag, just in case. She let herself out of her room and locked it again. She froze as the front door shuddered. The party was definitely on and it seemed like it was going to happen in the front yard and on the verandah if they weren't going to be invited in. That was as long as the front door held.

Ellie moved the curtain slightly and looked outside. She recognised some of the faces. She tensed when her gaze fell on a group of three men. Her gaze was drawn to one man in particular. Not good. She didn't want Tom here. She didn't even want to be here. Especially now she knew who was about. As much as she was glad Tom was coming to get her, she didn't want to constantly have him rescuing her. She knew she didn't need someone to rescue her every other day. Well, normally she didn't. Life was just completely screwed up lately. More so than usual.

When Tom pulled up in front of the house, Ellie unlocked the front door before he was even out of the car. There was no way she wanted him walking through the crowd on her front lawn. Before the door was barely open, people started pouring inside. Someone turned on the light. Ellie sighed. There was no way she was going to get them out of the house. She pushed her way through the door and into the yard.

"Well, if it isn't little Elizabeth."

Ellie tensed. "Scott. Been a while." She tried to walk past him but he grabbed her by the arm. Ellie glanced nervously at Tom who strode angrily towards them. Could things get any worse?

"Where you been hiding, Elizabeth?"

Ellie shrugged. "Oh, you know. Here and there. Life gets busy. Did you know Mum's in hospital? I bet she'd love to have a visit from you."

Tom reached her side. "Is there a problem here, Ellie?" He took her bags.

Ellie shook her head. "If you want to put my stuff in the car I'll be with you in a minute." She stared at him, willing him to do what she asked. She could deal with this on her own. She didn't need to be rescued.

He nodded abruptly and strode back to his car. Ellie turned to Scott who still held her arm tight. She forced herself to smile. "Like I said, life gets busy. I'll leave you to it. Got places to go."

"That your boyfriend, little Elizabeth?"

"Yeah."

"And here I thought you liked them a lot older." Scott smirked.

She nearly groaned when she saw Tom headed back towards her once he'd put her gear in his car. She smiled sweetly. "There's something to be said for youth, Scott. They can at least manage to do the deed when they try." She pushed hard against his chest with her free hand and pulled away from him when he stumbled. She spun and raced towards Tom, grabbing his hand as she reached him. "Get in the car and get me out of here."

They drove off to shouts from Scott and a beer bottle thrown after them. It smashed on the road. Ellie faced forward and closed her eyes for a second as she tried to push the scene with Scott from her mind. It was impossible. She buckled up.

"What was going on? Who were you talking to?"

"Just someone I don't get along with."

"Try again, Ellie."

"What do you want from me? To spill my guts about every little thing that has ever happened to me?" When he didn't answer, she yelled, "Well?"

Tom slowed the vehicle and pulled over onto the side of the road. He turned off the ignition and faced her. "Who was he?"

"I'm tired and I want to go to sleep."

"Elizabeth-"

"Don't ever call me that," she snarled. "Ever!"

"Ellie-"

"Do you understand? Never!" She pulled away from him when he reached for her.

Tom dropped his hands. "That man-"

"Scott. The bastard's name is Scott."

"Did Scott ever... " Tom looked away and swore.

"Having trouble asking? Is that because you don't want to know the answer?"

"I want to know."

"He never raped me. But not for lack of trying. He has a few drinks and thinks he's god's gift to women regardless of their age and believes no really means yes."

"How did you… that is…"

Ellie laughed bitterly. "Nice to see you at a loss for words for a change. It's usually your brother."

"Ellie-"

"I made avoiding him a talent. He's only ever there on weekends. And I'm never home then."

"You were today."

Ellie shrugged. "That was a mistake. I thought they'd get the message if there were no lights on. Seems like most of them are too thick to realise the party was cancelled."

"I guess it's no longer cancelled. You left the front door open."

"I wasn't stupid enough to think I could kick them out. There's nothing worth stealing. The TV is on the way out, the sofa probably should have gone to the tip years ago and not a single piece of cutlery or crockery matches. I locked my room. Hopefully that'll keep them out. But just in case, I brought my schoolbag and laptop."

"You shouldn't have to-"

Ellie pressed her fingers to Tom's lips. "Stop right there. This is my choice. Remember? It's the price I pay to run my own life. And I've been running it since I was thirteen. I'm not about to give that up." Not to mention someone had to look out for her mum. There was no one else to do it. But she doubted Tom would accept that reason.

Tom pulled her fingers away from his lips and linked his through them. "You're crazy."

Ellie tried to grin. "Lisbeth crazy?"

"Nah. Maybe Lizzie crazy though." He pulled her close, pressing her head against his chest. "You'll stay at my place every weekend."

"What about when you have swim meets?"

"Sam will be there. He only goes along to them if I beg him."

Ellie pulled back so she could meet his gaze. "Is this the same person who threatened to call the police if I didn't leave." She couldn't resist smiling.

"That was because Frankie's bride was at my place. I don't mind having you about." His lips met hers and the conversation was forgotten. He eventually pulled back slightly. "Ready to go? Or are we going to sit on the side of the road all night?"

Ellie laughed softly. "These bucket seats are killing me. Probably time to go. Besides you've got an early start tomorrow."

"Do you want to come too?"

"Ahh… well, who's going with you?"

"Mum."

"No." The word burst from her.

Tom laughed. "Chicken."

"Oh definitely. Your mum scares the hell out of me."

Tom shook his head. "You'll stand up to a complete bastard like Scott yet you shake at the thought of spending a day in my mother's company."

"Yep."

"And you call my brother odd."

"Shh. That's a state secret. No one but you and Lauren knows I'm odd."

"Good thing I get along with odd people then."

Ellie smiled, reaching out to rest her hand on Tom's thigh. "Yeah, good thing."

Chapter Twenty-One

Ellie stretched, rolling over in the bed. When she tried to see what time it was, a post it note was in the way. She reached out, removing it from the alarm clock. Nearly nine. No wonder she felt so well rested. She looked at the note.

'It was difficult to drag myself out of bed when you had yourself draped all over me. Sam volunteered to make you breakfast and do the hospital delivery. And right now, you're smiling in your sleep. Hope it's an interesting dream. Tom.'

Ellie smiled, climbing out of bed to put the note in her handbag. Her dreams had been interesting and Tom had featured in every one of them. Not that she was going to tell him that. She planned to leave him guessing.

Once she'd used the bathroom, she looked around for Sam. He wasn't anywhere downstairs. She heard a noise upstairs and decided to check up there for him. When she reached the upstairs lounge room, she paused and looked around. There was no one. Then she heard a noise in one of the kitchen cupboards. Ellie smiled, striding towards the sound. She smothered a scream when Gregory stood up.

"Have you come to help? Don't know where Sam is." Gregory pointed to the sink with his knife. "Wash your hands and julienne those carrots for me." He pushed a cutting board with four carrots towards her and pulled a knife from the cutting block, tucking it under the edge of her cutting board.

Ellie washed her hands and looked at the carrots. She grabbed the peeler Gregory handed her and gratefully began to peel them. She looked over to see what he was doing. She watched as he threw different seasonings as well as feta cheese, mayonnaise and other things she didn't recognise into a bowl and mixed them together. He was spreading the mixture over salmon fillets, that sat in a baking tray, by the time she'd peeled all the carrots. He sprinkled them with what looked like breadcrumbs then popped them in the oven.

Without a word, Gregory wiped off his hands and took one of the carrots and began chopping it on the board in front of him. Ellie managed to follow as far as turning the carrots into similar length rectangular chunks. Slicing them thinner looked beyond her capabilities. So she continued to trim them into rectangles and let Gregory finish turning them into thin strips.

She watched as he sliced through the carrots, making it look like he could have done it with his eyes closed. They were scraped off his board into a bowl. He shoved a colander at her and threw a handful of other vegetables into it.

"Wash them well."

Bemused, Ellie followed orders. She moved the colander back and forth under the tap a few times before she turned it off and shook them dry. She didn't know if she was doing the job correctly, but how hard could it be to wash vegetables? There were no heat sources involved so that was always a good start. She blinked as the colander was taken from her and the vegetables dumped onto Gregory's cutting board.

"Tablecloth is in the first drawer of the set of drawers closest to the dining room. Set the table for three." Gregory gestured with his knife again.

Ellie took out the ivory coloured tablecloth from the drawer and shook it out over the table. She tried to remember how Tom had set the table, wishing she'd paid more attention. But the food was what had taken up most of her interest.

"Not very talkative, are you?"

Ellie glanced back at Gregory.

"Serviettes are in the next drawer down. Don't worry about the rings."

"What are you cooking?" Ellie couldn't think of anything else to say.

"Feta crusted salmon served with fresh vegetables. I thought I should give it a test run before I let them serve it in the restaurant."

"Ahh… okay. Probably a good plan." What restaurant? She considered asking, but words failed her. Where was Sam? Ellie put three serviettes on the table, folding them into triangles. Next she added cutlery, leaving the knife, fork and spoon bundled together on each serviette. She didn't think it looked right, but it was better than not giving anyone cutlery.

"How long have you been dating Tom?"

"Ahh… a little while."

Gregory smiled. "Don't worry, it's not really any of my business. As long as you're over the age of consent. You are, aren't you?"

"Ahh… yeah."

"It's sixteen in Queensland."

"I know."

"You didn't sound so sure a moment ago."

Ellie rarely felt embarrassed, no matter who she was talking with or what the conversation was. But right now she wanted the floor to become Swiss cheese so she could disappear down a hole. She couldn't believe she was standing here having this conversation with her boyfriend's father. What was next? Safe sex? No way was she listening to that conversation. She'd already had that talk with her mum and it hadn't been anywhere near as bad as this discussion.

"Are you staying for dinner tonight?"

"Yeah." Ellie nodded. "If that's okay."

"Tom's welcome to invite who he wants. I just need to know how many I'm cooking for. Otherwise someone's going to end up hungry." He smiled.

Ellie nodded. "That makes sense." Finally, a safe topic.

"Are you staying all weekend?"

"Ahh..." what did she say to that? Where was Sam? She was going to kill him when she found him.

"Let me know when you figure it out. I'll be making all the meals this weekend."

"Tom said he's taking her home Sunday afternoon."

Ellie spun and could have raced over to Sam and

kissed him. Right before she killed him that was. Noticing his hair was damp, she made a mental note to check the pool first in future. "I was wondering where you'd disappeared to."

Gregory laughed. "Five minutes before the food is ready to go on the table. As always he has perfect timing."

"I wanted a swim."

"Well now you can take out three plates and help me clear up the mess on the kitchen benches." Gregory rinsed off dishes and stacked them in the dishwasher.

"It must be tough when you've got to cook at home. No kitchen help at your beck and call." Sam grinned as he threw the scraps in the bin.

"Be nice or I won't let you try my new recipe," Gregory warned.

Ellie couldn't help smiling at the way they interacted. She wished her father was just as approachable. Within minutes, the food was on the table and Ellie's mouth watered as she sat in her seat.

"Presentation?" Gregory looked towards Sam.

He eyed his plate. "Good colour mix with the vegetables. I like the texture of the salmon."

"It smells mouth watering. Are we going to eat or just admire it?" Ellie asked.

Gregory grinned. "Go ahead. This is a working meal for me."

Ellie picked up her fork. "This is breakfast for me." She had a mouthful of the salmon and closed her eyes as she ate it. When she opened her eyes, it was to find both Gregory and Sam staring at her. "What?"

"We're waiting on a verdict," Gregory said.

"Oh." She glanced at Sam. Maybe that's where he got his habit of staring at people from. Although Gregory's stare wasn't creepy, it just made her feel uncomfortable. Maybe Sam's stare wouldn't be so bad as he got older and didn't look so young. "It's nearly as good as pancakes, vanilla ice cream and maple syrup."

"What?" Gregory frowned.

Sam laughed. "It's her favourite meal."

"That's a dessert."

Ellie shook her head in disagreement. "Nope. Definitely a meal." She pointed to her plate with her fork. "And this would have to be up there pretty close to first place." She had another mouthful.

"How close?" Gregory asked.

Ellie looked at her plate thoughtfully. "If I could only pick one meal, I'd still have to go for the pancakes. But if I had an option of having seconds, I'd have firsts of this."

Gregory looked over to Sam. "Should I be worried that comment actually made sense to me?"

Sam nodded. "Absolutely."

"Last time I give my opinion." Ellie continued to eat her meal while Gregory and Sam started to discuss the food in minute detail. They became as involved in the discussion as she'd seen her father and Pamela involved in discussions over the latest news headlines. She enjoyed listening to them so much that when she finished eating, she sat back and watched.

Sam suddenly fell silent, turning towards her. "We're not boring you, are we?"

Ellie shook her head. "Not at all. Which surprises me since I can't think of anything more boring than cooking."

"Boring?" Gregory looked as stunned as someone who'd been told a bolt of lightning had struck their house and it was now a smouldering ruin.

"I have a tendency to set kitchens on fire."

"There's a fire extinguisher in the cupboard under the sink and one in the bottom drawer near the dining room," Gregory said.

"You have two?" Ellie stared at him.

"Of course. Some meals actually call for being set alight."

Ellie grinned. "And to think I've only ever got into trouble for setting food on fire."

"What was the first thing you set on fire?" Sam asked.

"Custard."

Sam and Gregory both echoed her word, disbelief on their faces.

Gregory shook his head. "How on earth did you set custard on fire?"

"I turned the stove up too high because it was taking so long to cook and then I got a text from a friend and had to reply. She sent one back and I forgot all about the custard as we kept sending messages to each other. Next thing I knew the girl cooking near me was screaming and there were flames coming out of the saucepan. I popped the lid on the saucepan and turned the element off but she still kept shrieking like a siren. At least I've always put my fires out."

Gregory shook his head again. "Custard."

Ellie nodded. "Yeah, but it didn't actually look like custard when I had to clean the saucepan. They ended up throwing it out. It wouldn't come clean. I had to replace it." She grinned. "So I took the one from home since it never got used."

"What do you eat if you never use a saucepan?" Gregory asked.

Sam shuddered. "You don't want to know. She might as well eat cardboard."

Ellie grinned. "Why do you think I love coming over here? I absolutely adore the food you cook." Her grin faded. "But I'm a little disappointed I didn't get my pancakes for breakfast."

Sam laughed. "I'll make them for you later, when you're ready for your lunch. A very late lunch."

"Excellent."

Sam pushed away from the table. "Do you want to go and play a game or something?"

Ellie nodded. "Sure, why not?" She picked up her plate, carrying it to the kitchen. Sam did the same. As soon as they'd rinsed and stacked them in the dishwasher, they headed downstairs.

Chapter Twenty-Two

The next few hours passed quickly as Ellie practised dying spectacularly. In the end, she dropped the controller on her lap and shook her head. "I think I'm better in the kitchen then I am at this game."

"That's a scary thought."

Ellie laughed. "Isn't it just? Now if only there was cooking involved. All the enemies would probably be barbequed. Then I'd win the game for sure."

"No doubt."

"I never thought to ask last night. What time does Tom get home?"

"Around six."

"That's ages away."

Sam stared at her for a few minutes. "Tom told me you had a legitimate reason for coming home with me that first weekend and I'm not to hassle you about it. Lauren said something similar."

"Is this your way of hassling me or are you telling me you're not going to hassle me?"

Sam shook his head. "I won't hassle. This is the last time I'll bring it up. But I do want to know. You wanted to know why I didn't ask you when you were first here. It was nice having a female actually talk to me and not act as if I didn't exist. I didn't want to scare you away when I was enjoying having you around."

"That's sweet."

"No, it's not. It's sad and pathetic." Sam shrugged. "But I'm sort of used to being that so it doesn't really bother me. I just can't work out why you came home with me. You're kind of popular. In an odd sort of way. Everyone seems to know you and says hello to you, well, everyone that counts that is. Yet you don't seem to really hang out with any of them. Just Lauren. I mean, you don't ignore them and you do things with them, but you seem like you don't really care if you're a part of their group or not. I'm not making sense, am I?"

Ellie smiled slightly. "You are. Just. I'll think about telling you. Or better yet, I'll think about letting Lauren tell you. It's not something I tell everyone. Lauren and Tom are the only ones who know the whole story. Well, Tom knows most of the story,

Lauren knows every little detail. But she won't be telling you every little detail if I let her tell you. Just the highlights."

"Okay." Sam nodded. "Do you want me to make you lunch or should I do the delivery first?"

"I'm not hungry yet. That food your father cooked might have sat light, but it's very filling."

"I'll tell him that. He'll like hearing that comment. Unless you wanted to tell him."

"Nah, it's okay. You can tell him. Do you mind if I use your computer while you're gone? I was thinking of catching up with emails." She considered getting her laptop out, but then she'd have to ask about accessing their internet. It seemed easier to use Sam's computer.

"You can use mine if you want, but Tom won't mind if you use his laptop."

"Thanks." Ellie grinned. "I didn't even think of it. I'll use his."

Sam turned off the PlayStation. "I'll make lunch when I'm back. Any messages for your mother?"

Ellie shook her head. "Not really. Oh and don't be offended if she calls you a geek when you tell her your name."

"Is that what you told her I was?"

"Not exactly. Heather was trying to find out where

I was staying and I said your name and then she wanted to know if you were my boyfriend and it all got a little complicated."

"I don't mind if you think that."

Ellie laughed. "You're odd and a little geeky but you're also really nice."

"And that makes me feel so much better when you say the last comment with a tone of surprise."

"Now I'm the one making a mess of explaining things. Maybe you better go before I completely insult you, which is the opposite of what I'm trying to do."

"Okay. Thank you, I guess."

"I wouldn't expect you to go quite that far. My compliment left a lot to be desired." Ellie rose to her feet. "Besides, I'm the one who should be saying thanks. For going to see my mum for me. Did Tom tell you which pub Mum's friend will be at with her drinks?"

"Yeah." He nodded. "I was a little surprised when Tom asked me, but I did some research online. Did you know–"

Ellie held up her hand to stop him. "Please. I don't want to talk about this right now."

Sam nodded. "That's okay." He headed for his room.

Ellie stared after him in surprise. She shook her head, wondering why she should be surprised. Sam was constantly doing the opposite of what she expected. She slowly made her way into Tom's room and turned on his laptop.

Once she'd answered emails, Ellie signed into her messenger. She signed in as offline since she really didn't want to talk to everyone. Just Lauren, if she was online. She grinned when she saw she was.

Ellie says: Hey.

Here kitty, kitty, kitty says: Was it odd being at home on a weekend.

Ellie says: Had a change of plans.

Here kitty, kitty, kitty says: What happened?

Ellie says: Party arrived anyway. Even Scott was there. Tom came and picked me up. Thought they were going to break down the front door with a battering ram.

Here kitty, kitty, kitty says: Oh no! You okay?

Ellie says: Yeah. Idiots. How could they not have realised there was no party when the place was locked up and no lights were on. Well, except for the verandah light, but it's permanently on.

They chatted for a while about how dense some

people were, trying to outdo each other with remembered incidents.

Here kitty, kitty, kitty says: I'm glad you ended up at Tom's place. Wish I was there too ;)

Ellie says: Sam's making a delivery to my mum.

Here kitty, kitty, kitty says: lol. Bet he gets a buzz out of that. He's probably picturing himself as some 1920s crime lord running illegal substances.

Ellie says: I've barely had time to talk to you this week about how the two of you are going.

Here kitty, kitty, kitty says: Where do I start. Have I told you I'm counting the days until he's seventeen? Normally it's my parents saying I'm not allowed to date. Odd to have it be his parents. Mine absolutely adore him. But he cooks like his dad. You should see his dad in action. He has such flair. Mum's always encouraging Sam to cook something when he comes over. Then she sits back and watches him like he's a TV show.

Ellie says: I have seen his dad cook.

Here kitty, kitty, kitty says: You finally gave in and watched one of his shows?

Ellie says: Nah, I helped him cook a meal earlier. Some salmon thing.

Here kitty, kitty, kitty says: Kitchen still standing?

Ellie says: Very funny!

Here kitty, kitty, kitty says: Still counting days till Sam's seventeen. You want me to tell you how many?

Ellie says: *rolls eyes* You're a sad, sad case.

Here kitty, kitty, kitty says: I know. Especially since I'm not likely to be able to sleep over like you get to.

Ellie says: I wish you could.

They chatted about Sam for a bit, or at least Lauren did while Ellie teased her, laughing at the similar comments Lauren made about her and Tom.

Here kitty, kitty, kitty says: Oh, brilliant news. I told mum you introduced me to Sam and she doesn't think you're so bad anymore. I'm still not allowed to have you over, but I am allowed to socialise with you if we're out in a crowd.

Ellie says: Wow. Before you know it I'll even be allowed to ring you again.

Here kitty, kitty, kitty says: lol. Brb

Ellie says: K.

Here kitty, kitty, kitty says: Back.

Ellie says: I was beginning to think you'd be gone forever.

Here kitty, kitty, kitty says: Sorry. That was Sam.

He's seen your mum. He wanted to ask me to come over to dinner tonight. Said that Tom could pick me up or I could bike back with him.

Ellie says: He was quick. It's only been about an hour and a half. What did you tell him?

Here kitty, kitty, kitty says: That I had to say goodbye to you. I'm riding over with him. We'll be there in about an hour.

Ellie says: Yes! Can't wait.

Here kitty, kitty, kitty says: Spending time with my two fave people in the world. What more could I want?

Ellie says: Sam turning seventeen ;)

Here kitty, kitty, kitty says: lol. Yep. I'll see you soon.

Ellie says: Buh-bye.

Here kitty, kitty, kitty says: Bibi.

While Ellie waited for Sam and Lauren to arrive, she changed into her bikini and went out to the pool. She was lazing in the shallow end when they turned up.

"Don't get out. We'll join you," Lauren called when Ellie started to climb out of the pool. "I'm dying of heat exhaustion. A swim is exactly what I need."

They splashed around for a while before they

ended up lazing about on the steps. "This is the perfect depth of water for laying about," Ellie said with a sigh. "You know, I was having so much fun I forgot all about lunch. I guess we might as well leave it for dessert now."

"And have a main meal as a dessert?" Sam teased.

Ellie grinned. "I know. Terrible, isn't it?"

Lauren played with Sam's hair. "I wonder what you'd look like with a mohawk." She spiked his hair up.

"Odd," Sam suggested.

"Or better yet, about three times the length of your brother's hair and lines shaved into it to make it look like a chess board. You'd have to dye it black and white too," Lauren said.

Ellie laughed. "You just want him to match you."

Lauren looked down at her own streaked hair. "Well, there is that too. But I also think it'd look cool."

"I don't know about that," Sam said.

"I bet I could convince you." Lauren moved in close to Sam.

"I'm sure you could." Before he could say another word, Lauren's lips met his and his eyes closed.

Ellie glanced away, spotting Teresa a moment

before she reached the edge of the patio. By then it was too late to warn Lauren.

"Sam!"

"Uhh… hello Mum."

"Your father told me both of the girls are staying for dinner."

Sam could only nod.

"Lauren can stay for dinner and then she's not welcome back until the seventh of January."

Lauren shook her head. "I'm sorry, Mrs Wallace. We were just mucking around. I mean… well not exactly… I was saying that a woman can always change a man's mind about something. We aren't… weren't… I-"

"Then this is your first and final warning, Lauren," Teresa said frostily.

"Yes, Mrs Wallace."

"If you even think along those lines you're back to waiting until January before you can visit again."

"Okay, Mrs Wallace. I'm terribly sorry about that. We were just-" Lauren gushed until she was interrupted by Teresa.

"Dinner will be ready in a little over an hour." Teresa strode inside.

"I'm so sorry, Sam." Lauren reached out to him, pulling her arm back before she could touch him.

Chapter Twenty-Three

Tom joined them in the pool with a grin for his brother. "I'm surprised you didn't try the old, I was just giving her mouth to mouth."

"I've obviously got poor timing," Lauren said.

"Depends on your point of view." Tom drew Ellie close to him.

"How did you do today?" Ellie leaned back against Tom.

"Not too bad. We won."

"Of course you did," Sam said. "You always win."

"It helps we've got a good team," Tom said.

Sam shook his head. "No need to be so modest, brother. You know you're the best swimmer."

Tom shrugged. "So what did you all get up to today?"

Tom was filled in on their day and then it was time for them to shower as the dinner hour was rapidly approaching. The start of the meal was filled with large silences and awkward pauses, but as the meal progressed things got better. After dinner, Sam promised to make dessert and bring it down and Lauren offered to help him. Tom and Ellie both retreated to Tom's bedroom.

"Are you going to tell me what you were dreaming about?"

"Hmm. That was so long ago it's hard to remember. I guess it couldn't have been too important since I can't remember a single dream."

"Not a single one, hey? How about two dreams? Or multiple dreams?"

Ellie lay stretched out on Tom's bed. "I'm glad you were already seventeen when I met you. It'd drive me crazy waiting for you to be old enough to have a girlfriend. Don't your parents realise that's a long time to wait? Poor Lauren."

Tom sat beside her on the bed, his hand capturing hers. "I would have snuck you in anyway rather than leave you at your place on a weekend."

"Does that mean I would have had to stay in your room all weekend?"

Tom grinned. "I can't see any problems with that idea. You want to pretend I'm still sixteen and hide out in here with me for the rest of the weekend?"

"Nice try." She reached out and pulled him to her so she could kiss him.

The rest of the world ceased to exist until there was a knock on Tom's bedroom door. When Ellie tried to push him away, Tom protested.

"That's probably dessert waiting for me," Ellie said.

Tom groaned and rolled over onto his back beside her. "Maybe after another few weeks of coming second to food I will have a self esteem problem."

Ellie laughed and leaned over to kiss him quickly. She pulled away when he reached out to hold her. "Dessert."

"Then we continue?"

Ellie shook her head. "Then we remind ourselves it's getting close to bedtime and I'm staying the night and expect you to behave yourself."

There was another knock on the door before Tom could say anything. He sighed and dragged himself off the bed, helping Ellie up. "Okay. You win. Dessert."

"Of course I win." Ellie rolled her eyes. "We're talking pancakes!"

Tom slid his arm around her waist and pretended to frown. "You think you should have them? I'm finding it a little harder to wrap my arm around you."

"If those pancakes weren't calling my name you'd have to die."

"I already am."

Ellie paused at the door to meet his gaze. She smiled when she saw the heat in his eyes. "Good. I wouldn't want to be the only one." She opened the door before he could answer her.

Lauren had her hand raised to knock again. "Finally. I was beginning to wonder if you'd checked out of reality."

"Forget that pancakes, vanilla ice cream and maple syrup are waiting for me? Never."

* * *

Ellie sat quietly in the car beside Tom on Sunday afternoon. He'd given up trying to talk to her. Her grunts and single syllable answers hadn't been very helpful in keeping the conversation going. But she couldn't do anything about that. She was worried about what she'd find. Worried she might not even have a home left. And then where would she go? It wasn't like she could move in with Tom permanently. Their relationship was still too new to even expect that. Besides, who would look after her mum if she wasn't there?

"You want to tell me what's wrong, Ellie?"

She shook her head. "I don't want to talk about anything right now."

"It's a really annoying habit you have."

"What?"

"Shutting everyone out and ignoring the rest of the world when it's not going according to your plan."

Ellie looked out the window. What could she say? It was true. She did have a tendency to clam up when life went to pieces around her. That was her way of dealing with it. He was just going to have to get over his problem with it.

"Come on, Ellie. I can't help you if I don't know what's going on."

"Maybe I don't need your help. You don't have to play knight rescuing a damsel in distress every minute of the day. I can look after myself, you know."

"Of course I know. But that doesn't mean you have to. You can accept help from other people without being weak."

Ellie continued to look out the window, watching as the neighbourhood deteriorated. "I'm worried my house might be more trashed than usual."

"So we'll deal with it."

"What if it's burned to the ground?"

"We see if there's any coals left to toast marshmallows on?"

Ellie laughed weakly as they turned into her street. "Well, I guess I can't see any smoke in the sky. But that doesn't mean anything."

"Whatever it is, you'll deal with it. I have complete faith in your ability to deal with anything."

"Thank you." Ellie fell silent again, but this time it didn't seem as uncomfortable. Her gaze focused on her home when they pulled up in front of it. The front door was closed and the verandah light was still on. It looked as dilapidated as it always did. There were several empty bottles in the front yard, that usually didn't get left there. Other than that, everything looked normal. "Pull up in front of the neighbour's house."

Tom drove along a bit further and turned the engine off. He took her bags and a full plastic grocery bag off the backseat, waiting until Ellie was out of the car before he locked it.

Ellie tried the front door and found it unlocked. She swung the door open and was relieved to see everything looked normal. Well, normal for a Sunday afternoon. "What's in the plastic bag?"

Tom shook his head. "I'll tell you later. You want to unlock your room so I can put this stuff down.

There doesn't look to be one clean spot out here today."

As soon as they'd put Ellie's gear in the bedroom and Tom had stashed the plastic bag in the fridge they began to clean up. The first thing they did was close all the curtains in case Heather turned up unexpectedly. Once the house was back to normal, Tom glanced around the living area.

"Where do you eat your meals?"

Ellie pointed to the small space beside the kitchen that was empty. "Occasionally I throw a picnic blanket on the floor in the dining area, but mostly I either sit on the island bench or at my computer desk."

"Do you want to grab the picnic blanket?"

"It's not a real picnic blanket. It's a normal blanket that's too thin to be much use in winter."

Tom shrugged. "Doesn't matter. It'll do."

Ellie grabbed the blanket out of her room and laid it on the floor. She watched as Tom took the plastic bag from the fridge and set containers on the blanket. In the bottom of the bag was a candle in a holder. He lit it with a lighter he drew from his pocket.

Ellie laughed. "Do you think it'll burn better now it's cold?"

Tom grinned. "I didn't want you to see it."

"So what's all this in aid of?" Ellie's hand gestured towards the blanket.

"Sam made us dinner. There should be enough food here for breakfast and lunch tomorrow."

"I should be annoyed he thinks I can't feed myself." She opened one of the containers and inhaled. "But I can't resist his food."

"He made sure it was food that could be served cold."

Ellie grinned as she grabbed cutlery. She handed some to Tom. After a mouthful, she turned to him. "Sometimes I swear I could compete against Midas."

"I'm not following."

"Everything he touched turned to gold. This is better than gold. And to think picking Sam was a half random act. Sometimes I'm amazed at my luck."

"And what do you call having an alcoholic for a mother?"

Ellie glared at him. "Don't ruin the evening."

"Come on Ellie, I'm curious."

"Balance."

"What?" Tom frowned then shook his head. "No, I still can't comprehend that."

"Everyone has good and bad in their life. They balance each other out. With how extremely lucky I am in other things there has to be some major crap in there somewhere."

Tom stared at her for a minute. "I have told you how odd I think you are, haven't I?"

Ellie nodded. "Yep."

"Just wanted to make sure." He picked up another container and sank his fork into the food.

Chapter Twenty-Four

At the end of lunch on Thursday, Lauren dragged
Ellie to the toilets so she could talk to her without
Sam overhearing them. As soon as she'd made sure
the room was empty, Lauren turned to Ellie.

"I need you to talk Tom into taking us all to the
beach on Saturday."

"Why can't you ask him?"

"Because I'm being horribly shallow and you know
what I'm like when I have an ulterior motive."

"What's going on, Lauren?"

"Michelle's been making comments about how
much Sam has been hanging around us. You know
how they all call him Baby Face. If it wasn't for
Tom I bet they'd hassle him worse. But Tom's really
popular so they kind of leave his brother alone. It'll
probably be different next year when Tom's at uni. I
worry about what'll happen then. I'm trying to work

out how to make Sam more acceptable before that happens."

"And how are you doing that?"

"I've let a few people try his cooking and I need to get him to the beach on Saturday."

Ellie frowned. "I'm not sure how the beach is going to help."

"Because Michelle has organised for everyone to meet up at the beach Saturday."

"Why didn't I hear anything about it?"

Lauren grinned. "Gee, I don't know. Might have something to do with how focused you've been on a certain person."

Ellie returned her grin. "Can you blame me?"

Lauren shook her head. "No, but I need you to use some of that focus to help me with Sam. I want us to make him… well not popular, but at least so no one wants to pick on him."

"Hmm. I guess. But how is getting him to the beach going to help?"

"Seriously. I worry about you sometimes. That boy has a chest to make your heart stop beating. If only I could keep his shirt off all the time. Not a single female would even notice his baby face."

"The guys would."

"Only if they weren't gay."

Ellie laughed. "You are getting desperate with your plans."

"There isn't much time left–" Lauren broke off as the door opened and two girls walked in.

"We'll sort it out," Ellie said.

"I hope so."

The bell went and they stepped outside. Ellie froze when she heard her name over the PA system.

"Would Elizabeth Malloy please report to the office?"

"I haven't done anything. Why would they want me?"

Lauren shrugged. "You don't think it's something to do with your mum, do you?"

Ellie shook her head. "I doubt it. Tom said she looked heaps better when he visited her yesterday. Guess I better get it over and done with."

"I'll come with you."

"Thanks, Lauren." They were nearly there when Ellie stopped suddenly. "Oh no. What if it's Heather? Mum said she hasn't been at the hospital for two days. Not that I'm counting on that to continue. But what if she's decided to track me down here?"

"I'll go and see for you."

"You don't know what she looks like."

Lauren pulled out her phone. "I'll take a photo of

every stranger hanging out in the office. Unless she's not at the front desk. I'm definitely not going inside."

"I wouldn't ask you to. Just take photos of anyone you can see through the windows."

"Back in a sec."

Ellie moved off the path and stood close to the trunk of a tree. The grounds were rapidly emptying as students headed to their next class. She didn't want to be questioned about why she was hanging around doing nothing. When she saw Lauren running towards her, she stepped away from the tree.

"Only two strangers." Lauren handed her phone over.

Ellie swore. "This one. This is Heather." She turned the phone so Lauren could see the woman in the second photo she'd taken. Panic raced through her, making her feel five-years-old again. And helpless. "I've got to get out of here."

"You'll be sprung for ditching school."

"I'll figure something out."

"Like what?"

She wasn't five and she wasn't helpless. Panic receded and she hatched a plan. "Any teacher asks, my period came unexpectedly and someone noticed the blood on my skirt and was paying out on me. Tell them I took off home, embarrassed."

"I hope you don't expect me to tell male teachers."

Ellie nodded. "You'll live."

"Not if I die of embarrassment."

"I've got to run."

"Be careful."

"I will. All this will be over Monday. Mum comes home then." At least she hoped it'd be over then. Surely Heather wouldn't have any reason to keep hassling her once her mum came home.

Lauren rolled her eyes. "Until the next disaster."

"But something good always comes out of them." Ellie waved as she ran to collect her schoolbag and head home. She sent a text to Tom the moment she was safe at home. He didn't take long to reply.

Want me to drop around when school's over?

No. All good. Staying home tomorrow.

I'll catch you online later.

Ellie smiled and put her phone on the bedside drawers. She guessed she might as well kill some time catching up on her assignments.

* * *

Hurry up January says: You are in so much trouble at school.

Ellie says: What happened?

Hurry up January says: They dragged me out of class since they somehow know we hang out together. Makes you wonder if there are spies at our school reporting on everything we do and say.

Ellie says: Might be bugs.

Hurry up January says: And spy cam.

Ellie says: lol. Get back on track. What happened?

Hurry up January says: Heather was there and she had a million questions for me. Seriously, I was wondering if she was planning on torture next.

Ellie says: She's obsessed. I really hate that woman.

Hurry up January says: Me too.

Hurry up January says: You still there?

Ellie says: Thinking.

Hurry up January says: About?

Ellie says: Options.

Hurry up January says: And?

Hurry up January says: Stop killing me. Tell me everything. How long do you need to figure out a plan?

Ellie says: Give me a minute.

Hurry up January says: I'm still waiting. It's been over a minute.

Ellie says: I'm not coming to school tomorrow.

Hurry up January says: That doesn't sound like much of a plan.

Ellie says: I'll go see my doctor and get a certificate. Tell him I've got really bad cramps.

Hurry up January says: Let's hope he doesn't expect you to prove you've got them.

Ellie says: Nah, he thinks I'm the sweetest kid out.

Hurry up January says: I swear you could trick a lie detector.

Ellie says: Who me? *looks angelic and innocent*

Hurry up January says: *while kicking her forked tail behind her with her cloven hooves*

Ellie says: lol.

Hurry up January says: How will that help you get out of trouble at school?

Ellie says: Because I'll see the vice principal. He's not good at dealing with tears.

Hurry up January says: Harsh.

Ellie says: Yep and I'll tell him how stressful it's been with Mum in hospital and how it all got too much for me and then I was in dreadful pain from cramps and wasn't thinking clearly… he'll be telling me to take a week off before I'm finished with him. : D

Hurry up January says: Should I get a sympathy card ready to send to him for when you're finished with him?

Ellie says: : D

Hurry up January says: Well, if anyone can pull it off, it'd be you.

Ellie says: Yep.

Ellie says: Hey, I've g2g. Tom's trying to chat to me.

Hurry up January says: That's Okay. Sam's chatting to me : D

Ellie says: Oh, before I forget, don't you want a kitten anymore?

Hurry up January says: Yeah, but it isn't my number one priority : D

Ellie says: lol. I don't think January is going to come any quicker even if you do your 'think positive' trick. It hasn't worked for a kitten.

Hurry up January says: I know, but I've gotta try something.

Ellie says: Luck.

Hurry up January says: Thanks.

Ellie says: Buh-bye.

Hurry up January says: Bibi.

Chapter Twenty-Five

Ellie read over what Tom had written. Grinning, she started typing again.

TW says: Hey.

TW says: I know you're about. Even though you're set as offline.

TW says: Hurry up and finish talking to Lauren.

TW says: Would it kill you to acknowledge that I'm chatting to you.

Ellie says: brb.

TW says: Most people can cope with two conversations at once.

TW says: It's called multitasking.

TW says: Hurry up!

Ellie says: So impatient. : D

TW says: Impatient! You've got to learn how to deal with more than one conversation at a time.

Ellie says: Nope. You'll just have to learn patience.
: D

TW says: So why did you take off early?

Ellie says: Heather turned up at school looking for me.

TW says: Why couldn't you have said that instead of 'gone home sick'.

Ellie says: Because that was my official excuse.

TW says: Give me the real reason in future. And the official one too of course.

Ellie says: Want to go to the beach on Saturday?

TW says: Well that was certainly a major topic change.

Ellie says: Well?

TW says: Why?

Ellie says: Don't you like going to the beach?

TW says: I don't know anyone who hates it.

Ellie says: Do you have anything else planned for Saturday?

TW says: Sleeping in?

Ellie says: We can go to bed early Friday night.

TW says: There's a party I want to go to.

Ellie says: So we leave around midnight.

TW says: What's happening at the beach?

Ellie says: People from my grade are meeting up. I want to go, but I want to spend the day with you too.

TW says: Sure it isn't because I make a good chauffeur?

Ellie says: Nah, I can catch a lift with one of the others going.

TW says: No other ulterior motives?

Ellie says: You look good in boardies : D

TW says: lol. Sure, why not.

Ellie says: Can Sam and Lauren come too?

TW says: If they want.

Ellie says: Can Sam provide lunch?

TW says: Ahh, that's why you're inviting us, isn't it?

Ellie says: Well, it was a consideration. It wasn't like I could just ask Sam to pack up a lunch for me and not take either of you along.

TW says: Really? Does that mean you considered it?

Ellie says: Hmmm.

Ellie says: Interesting question.

Ellie says: Don't know if I should answer it…

TW says: Just remember you want me to pick you up tomorrow afternoon when school is out so you can spend the weekend at my place.

Ellie says: I could catch a bus.

TW says: But would I let you in?

Ellie says: Yep : D

TW says: Okay, you win. Of course I would.

Ellie says: We'll call it a tie. I didn't want to go to the beach unless you were coming too.

TW says: Was that so hard to tell me?

Ellie says: Excruciating.

TW says: I just asked Sam and he said yes to both questions.

Ellie says: Both?

TW says: He's coming and he'll make lunch. Any preferences?

Ellie says: Well…

TW says: Not pancakes.

Ellie says: : (

TW says: You'll live. It's not beach food anyway.

Ellie says: Fine. Tell him to surprise me. Is he asking Lauren? Since I'm no good at multitasking : P

TW says: Yeah. She's coming.

Ellie says: Great.

TW says: I've g2g. Just wanted to see how you were before I head to the pool.

Ellie says: Sorry. Will give you both excuses next time.

TW says: Please.

Ellie says: You be online later?

TW says: Eight?

Ellie says: I'll catch you then.

TW says: K. Later.
Ellie says: Buh-bye.

* * *

Ellie and Tom were parked in front of Lauren's house. They waited for Sam to bring her out. Ellie didn't want to test Lauren's parents' change of mind over letting Lauren socialise with her only when they were in a group. She grinned when she saw Lauren burst out her front door, half dragging Sam with her. He was looking over his shoulder, nodding to Lauren's mother who'd followed them out. Lauren waved to her mother before she reached the car, pulling the door open.

"I thought we'd never get out of there. Just ignore her Sam. She'll keep talking otherwise." Lauren tugged on Sam's hand, dragging him into the car.

Ellie laughed. "But you know how she adores Sam."

Sam blushed as he got in the car, closing the door. "It's not so much me as my father. She can't stop asking me questions about him."

"I bet she's already planning the wedding between the two of you." Ellie grinned when Sam went even redder.

"Behave." Tom dropped his hand on Ellie's thigh.

"Oh, I am. I'm on my best behaviour today. I even gave Lisbeth the day off."

"But what about Lizzie?" Tom asked.

"You can't have everything." She linked her fingers through Tom's and glanced in the back. "Awfully quiet in there. No getting x-rated. My innocent eyes couldn't cope."

"Innocent! Yeah right," Lauren said. "Keep your eyes forward and you won't have a problem."

Ellie laughed. "Just give me a minute to get my phone out and start recording. I could make a fortune online."

Tom's hand tightened on hers. "You're in a good mood today."

"Yep. I like going to the beach."

"Hmm."

Ellie glanced at Tom. "What?"

"Why do I think you've got something else planned?"

Ellie shrugged. "Because you're permanently suspicious?"

"No, because you look like you're up to something. Trouble."

"The way you're talking you'd think I was always planning something." Lauren laughed and Ellie turned so she could grin at her friend. "And no comments from you." She turned back to Tom. "I don't always go out of my way to plan trouble. It tends to find me. I'm like a magnet for it."

"Sure."

"The whole world is a critic." She shook her head sadly. "I don't know how I put up with all of you."

"Because we feed you?" Tom suggested.

"Well… that's a good point." Ellie grinned at Tom when he glanced at her. "Aren't you looking forward to a day at the beach?"

"Yeah."

"Well there you go. So am I." And making sure Michelle and her friends set their sights on someone else to pick on. But that was between her and Lauren. Tom didn't need to know every single thought she had. Well, maybe she'd tell him. She'd think about it.

* * *

Ellie looked around the beach at the crowd. It seemed like half her grade was there. Although that was probably an exaggeration. She spotted Michelle and waved to her with a friendly smile.

Lauren came to stand beside her. "Are we doing the right thing?"

Ellie watched Tom and Sam who were setting up a beach umbrella and blankets. "Yes. By the time today ends, every female in our grade is going to be interested in Sam."

"Not too interested," Lauren protested.

"Don't you trust him?"

"Why would he want me if someone like Michelle was throwing themselves at him? She's bikini-model-gorgeous."

Ellie dropped her arm around Lauren's shoulders. "Don't sweat it. He's not going to look at anyone other than you. He adores you. You're his first girlfriend. He worships the ground you walk on."

"I think Michelle wants to talk to you."

"Yeah. Give me a couple of minutes. And get our boys half naked for me." Ellie grinned. "Tell Tom I'll meet him in the surf."

"I've been wondering if I've done the right thing ever since Sam invited me." Lauren glanced towards Michelle again. "Her tongue is sharper than every knife in Gregory's kitchen."

"Leave her to me. You just work on having a good day and seeing that Sam enjoys himself. And make sure he gets his shirt off when I'm over with Michelle. Even if you have to strip it off him."

Lauren giggled. "Like that's going to be a real hardship."

"I know. It's a tough job, but I'm relying on you." With a wink to her friend, Ellie pulled her dress over her head and handed it to Lauren. She'd worn her bikini under her dress to make it easier to hit the water as soon as possible. A quick wave to Tom, who was still helping Sam set up their spot, and she strode towards Michelle.

"I couldn't believe it when you turned up with Tom. There's been so much talk about you pair and everyone is wondering what's going on." Michelle stared past Ellie's shoulder at Tom.

"Isn't he just die-in-his-arms gorgeous?" Ellie couldn't resist another glance at him.

"How on earth did you manage to get your claws into him? I swear every single girl in our grade, oh what am I talking about, every single girl at our school is absolutely green."

"Well, I don't know about that. I'm sure not every girl. But yeah, I'm not surprised. He was certainly a hard one to catch."

"How did you do it? And how on earth do you manage to put up with his brother? Sam is such a loser."

Ellie leaned in close to Michelle and dropped her voice. "Just between you and me."

"Yes?"

"Him and his brother are extremely close. Best friends. I made friends with Sam first."

Michelle drew back in surprise. "Get outta here! Really?"

Ellie nodded. "Absolutely true."

"Wow. You'd never think it when you see them together at school."

"Only because they've got different interests. But they spend heaps of time with each other and they get along better than any siblings I've ever known."

"Wow." Michelle looked over towards Tom and Sam again.

Ellie grinned when Lauren removed Sam's shirt and Michelle grabbed her arm with a sudden indrawn breath. She managed to stay silent for a few minutes longer, but when Lauren started to rub sunscreen on Sam, Michelle's grip tightened on her arm. "Are you all right? You've gone awfully quiet." She managed to make her expression suitably serious.

Michelle met her gaze. "Baby Face has a body."

"Of course he does. You need something to attach a head to."

Michelle rolled her eyes. "Abs, muscles, my god,

who'd think that was hidden under his shirt. Where'd he get it?"

"I told you, him and Tom are best friends. He trains with his brother on the weekend to keep him company."

"Pity he looks like he's barely thirteen and can't string more than two words together."

Ellie shrugged. "And a guy who prefers to listen is a problem because?"

Michelle grinned. "Of course it's not a problem. But is that really how you hooked up with Tom?"

Ellie nodded. "Yep."

"How long have you been with Tom?"

Ellie shrugged. "A couple of weeks or there about. Why?"

"Oh, you poor thing. Isn't five weeks his longest relationship?"

"Who wants to worry about something like that?" Ellie waved the concern away. "I'm planning to enjoy every second I do have with him."

Michelle watched Tom as he ditched his shirt and put sunscreen on his chest. "How can you stand to let him out of your reach? You never know who might snatch him away from you."

Ellie shrugged. "If I've got to keep that close a watch on him then I'm not interested."

"You're crazy. Oh. Oh. He's coming this way."

Ellie smiled as Tom walked towards her, after he'd poured more sunscreen in his hand. "Have a problem?" she asked when he reached her.

"I could have asked Lauren to help out, but she seemed a little preoccupied."

"I can help," Michelle hurriedly offered.

"Have you met Michelle before, Tom?"

"Not that I recall."

Ellie took some of the sunscreen from his hand. "She goes to our school." She started to rub the sunscreen into his back.

Before Michelle could say anything else, David joined their group. "What is everyone doing standing around? This is a beach. We should be hitting the waves."

Ellie stepped back in front of Tom. "All done."

Tom held up his hand that still had sunscreen in it. "Need any?"

"Might as well. Although I smeared it all over myself before we left this morning."

"Now that wasn't very nice of you. I thought that was meant to be my job." Tom spread the sunscreen between both his hands before he ran them down her arms.

"We?" Michelle looked between each of them.

Ellie nodded. "I've been staying at Tom's place on the weekend." Her gaze shifted to David. "We're ready to hit the waves. You coming, David?"

"No fear."

Ellie linked her fingers through Tom's. "I wish I'd brought a body board with me. It looks great out there today."

"I brought my surfboard," David offered.

Ellie shook her head and laughed. "No way. I want to enjoy myself not spend my day being dumped."

"If you don't mind, I'll borrow it later," Tom said.

Michelle hurried to join them. "You surf?" Her gaze was glued to Tom, who shrugged in answer.

"No probs. Give me a yell when you want a go," David said.

They reached the water's edge and splashed into the shallows. Ellie waved to Lauren and Sam who were already in the water. Lauren gestured her over with a grin. Ellie nodded and turned to Tom. "Feel like a swim?" She grinned.

Tom laughed. "Stupid question."

They ran through the shallows towards deeper water.

Chapter Twenty-Six

By the middle of the day Ellie was glad to lie under the shade of the beach umbrella. She was ready for a break from the water but her lips were permanently curved in a smile. She was also dying to see what food Sam had prepared for lunch. He didn't disappoint her.

Once she'd eaten, she lay back and closed her eyes for a bit, falling asleep. The next thing she knew, she was being kissed by Tom. Her eyes slowly opened and he drew back to smile down at her.

"You're not going to sleep the whole day away are you?"

"The beach always does that to me. How long was I asleep?"

"Nearly two hours. You're missing all the fun."

"Don't listen to him, Ellie. He crashed out too. And he'd still be sleeping if someone inviting him to play beach volleyball hadn't woken him. They've got a net set up and everything," Lauren said.

"I don't know. I can't trust a word you say." Ellie shook her head with an appropriately sad expression.

"Hmm. I know exactly how you feel."

Ellie laughed. "So, are you going to play?"

"Come join us?"

"Does it involve moving much?"

Tom lightly kissed her. "Come play and you can have afternoon tea when the game's over. If you don't play you'll never find out what I brought for you."

"Will I like it?"

"You'll hate yourself if you miss out on it."

Ellie sat up. "All right. Where's the game?"

The game was fairly informal and the aim was to have fun rather than score points. When everyone started to head back to the water to cool off, Tom took Ellie to the beach umbrella. Lauren and Sam were nowhere to be seen.

"Wait here."

"Where are you going?" Ellie sat on the blanket.

Tom smiled. "It's a surprise."

"A food surprise?"

Tom nodded.

"The one you were telling me about?"

"The sooner you quit with the questions the quicker I'll be back and you can have your surprise."

Ellie mimicked zipping her lips. She grinned when Tom started to walk away, heading for the shop across the road from the beach. She eyed the large esky that sat under the umbrella with her. It was tempting. And she was all alone. A quick peek and no one would know any different. Ellie nearly groaned when Michelle joined her on the blanket.

"Where's Tom? Did he ditch you already?"

Ellie smiled, leaning forward to confide, "He's planned a surprise for me."

"Really?" Michelle glanced around. "Then where is he?"

"How would I know? Something to do with the surprise."

"Oh. Oh. He's coming now. And he's carrying something in a plastic bag. It doesn't look very big. It can't be much of a surprise."

Ellie's smile slipped. She wanted to tell Michelle where to go, but knew that was social suicide. "It's food, Michelle."

Michelle frowned. "How can food be a surprise?"

"Because they cook."

"Who does?"

"Tom's family. I guess you could call it a family hobby."

Michelle looked at her in surprise. "You can't cook at all. Does he know?"

"Yep and he thinks it's funny."

"Are you sure?"

Ellie nodded. "Absolutely." She smiled at Tom as he sat by the esky. "You took your time. I was beginning to wonder if you'd got lost."

"Anticipation improves everything."

"I don't know about that. All my wait seems to have done is made me hungrier."

"Ellie said your family cooks as a hobby. If you made her something to eat, why did you need to go to the shop?"

Ellie tried to hold back the annoyance Michelle's interruption caused. It suddenly evaporated as she saw what Tom took out of the esky and put in a bowl. "Oh, you didn't. I can't believe it." She grinned when he pulled a small tub of vanilla ice cream out of the plastic bag. "You are perfect."

"You did request pancakes, vanilla ice cream and maple syrup." Tom poured the maple syrup and handed the bowl to Ellie.

"Why would you want to eat something like that at the beach? That's weird," Michelle said.

"It was a joke," Tom said shortly.

"Oh. That makes more sense."

Ellie ignored Michelle as she took a bite. She looked over to Tom who watched her with a similar expression to what she'd seen on his brother and father's face. She broke off a piece of the pancake and ate it plain. "It's different."

"Is that good or bad?" Tom asked.

"Definitely good. I don't know what Sam did to it, but it's even better than ever." Ellie took another mouthful.

Tom smiled. "I made it."

Ellie pointed at him. "You are going to cook me a meal."

"Really, Ellie, that's no way to talk to someone who's just gone out of their way to make you food." Michelle rolled her eyes. "You're meant to show a little gratitude."

Tom grinned at Ellie. "Now Michelle has pointed it out, I've noticed you haven't thanked me for all the effort I went to. I had to sneak upstairs really early in the morning so you wouldn't know what I was up to."

"If it's gratitude you're looking for I'll try and do my best. Let me see." Ellie looked thoughtful as she had another mouthful. "I'm going to marry you and become as big as a house."

"Ellie!" Michelle looked utterly shocked.

Tom laughed. "I can't take a proposal seriously unless it's done on one knee with a ring held out."

"Nope, can't do that. I'm too busy eating this divine meal."

Michelle shook her head. "I'd like to try some. It's only a pancake. Really, Ellie, you're being extremely weird about it."

Ellie barely managed not to snarl at Michelle. Why did she have to stick around and ruin this moment?

Tom pointed behind Michelle. "I think someone is trying to get your attention over there." When Michelle started to turn away, he spoke again. "We'll catch up with you in the water. We should be back in soon. You'll probably want to put more sunscreen on before you go in again. You're starting to look a little pink. I'd hate to see you get sunburned."

"Thank you, Tom. That's thoughtful of you to notice." Michelle rose to her feet. "I'll see you both soon."

The moment Michelle was out of earshot, Tom turned to Ellie. "What do you see in that girl?"

"You really don't want to know."

"Because?"

"It's not very nice."

"Then why put up with her?"

"Because offending her is like insulting the king or queen of a country. I'd have to change my name and relocate overseas."

Tom laughed. "I'm sure it can't be that bad."

"Michelle is one of the main people who teases your brother." Ellie put her hand on Tom's arm when he looked like he'd rise to his feet. "Be nice to her."

"Why would I be nice to that bitch?"

"Because it's all under control."

"Is that what today was all about? The trouble you were planning?"

Ellie shrugged. "Sort of."

"Come on, Ellie. You know I'll drag it out of you eventually."

Ellie sighed and had another mouthful of her food. It was nearly finished. She eyed the esky. "Do you have any more in there? Surely you didn't cook just one."

"The rest are at home. No changing the subject."

Ellie finished eating her pancake and handed the bowl to Tom. "Lauren was really worried about you not being at school next year to reduce some of the bullying. Neither of us are popular enough that it'd make a difference in the way Sam's treated."

"So Lauren was in on this too?"

Ellie shook her head. "Not really. I told her I'd take care of it." She smiled. "Unlike some people she has complete faith in my plans."

"So what is the plan?"

"You have to keep being nice to Michelle and everything else will fall into place."

"Ellie."

She couldn't miss the warning in his tone. "I really hate having to explain all the tiny details. People usually look at me like I'm some slime left behind in a pond that's dried up."

"Unlike most people I already know you don't mind manipulating and lying to make things go the way you want them to. You might as well tell me everything."

"Michelle pointed out that your longest relationship is five weeks. But I already knew that."

"Ours will be longer."

"How do you know?"

"Because you don't spend every minute of the day and night being self centred and shallow. And I spend nearly every weekend peeling away all the new layers to find out what you're up to."

Ellie laughed, thinking of Lauren's comment about

Easter eggs in clothes. "Okay, but if you mess up my plan I'm going to be very annoyed with you."

"You never know, I might even be able to improve on it."

"I told her Sam is your best friend and I hooked up with you by becoming his friend. I explained that you spend a lot of your weekends with your brother."

"How is that going to get her to lay off him?"

Ellie moved closer to Tom and smiled up at him. "Because she's expecting us to be only short term, so she's going to become friends with Sam. When she eventually gives up on you she won't be able to suddenly turn on Sam without looking like a complete bitch. Unless Sam does something utterly stupid, which I can't see him doing because he's shy rather than an idiot. So she'll have to stay friendly towards him. And if Michelle is friends with him, all her friends will be and all the guys who desperately want to hook up with her."

"And I thought you were leaving Lisbeth at home today."

Ellie grinned. "She obviously snuck along."

"So how do I thank you for looking out for my little brother?"

"You don't. That was an example of me being self centred and shallow."

Tom shook his head. "Now you've really lost me."

Ellie sighed. "And I guess that means you're expecting an explanation." She wasn't happy to see Tom nod. "Okay. Lauren is my best friend. If something upsets her, it upsets me. And if someone is picking on her, they'll eventually start on me, because I can't stand back and let them. And if she stays with your brother that will happen with the way he's treated. So I'm just looking out for myself."

Tom shook his head. "No. You're looking out for your friend. That isn't shallow." He groaned.

"What?"

"Are you sure I have to be nice to the queen bitch?"

Ellie laughed. "Now that's a name I can enjoy using. Yes, you do. Why?"

"Because she's heading for the water and waving us over."

"We can drown our sorrows with pancakes, vanilla ice cream and maple syrup when we get home."

Tom laughed and rose to his feet, pulling Ellie with him. "No wonder you fit into my family so well. That's exactly the way we think about food. A solution to every problem."

Chapter Twenty-Seven

Ellie walked down the corridor to her mum's hospital room. Tom waited out the front to give them a lift home. She was later then she'd planned to be, but she'd wanted to do the grocery shopping first. Knowing what the first weekend her mum had been in hospital had been like, she'd left the door unlocked so it didn't get busted open when the party had arrived. And it had arrived. Sunday afternoon had been spent doing the usual clean up. It also meant the bit of food she'd left behind had been eaten.

Ellie froze in the doorway of her mum's room. She quickly stepped into the room when Heather turned towards her. She wanted to demand what she was doing here, but didn't think that was the best tactic.

"Hello, Heather. I didn't imagine I'd see you here today."

"I'm sure you didn't, Elizabeth."

She barely managed to stop herself from demanding that Heather stop calling her that name. Only three people did. Her father, Pamela and Scott.

"I've been stuck with her for over an hour. You'd think she'd have more important things to do than hang out here with me," Sharon muttered.

Ellie smiled. "That was nice of you to keep Mum company while she waited for me."

"I know you're not an imbecile, Elizabeth. And since I'm not either, you can drop the games. You've managed to avoid me for the past fortnight, which is quite an accomplishment."

Ellie shook her head and let her mouth fall open slightly while a frown marred her forehead. "I think you're giving me more credit than I deserve. I'm sorry you've felt like I've been avoiding you. It's been a busy couple of weeks for me and of course I wasn't feeling well Thursday and Friday so I spent the weekend catching up on all I would have normally done those days."

"I tried to tell her you'd have no reason to avoid her." Sharon got to her feet with the help of the crutches beside her.

Ellie was instantly at her mum's side. "You need any help, Mum?"

"Just grab my bag." Sharon headed for the doorway.

"You will understand I have some concerns about your living arrangements after the way you've avoided me the past fortnight. And what I have heard from your stepmother leaves me with even more concerns." Heather walked beside Ellie down the corridor.

"You're welcome to come and check them out if you want. We live in an average house in an average neighbourhood. We're shocking gardeners but we couldn't find a house with a fake lawn. Don't you think that'd be much easier to look after? Although I'm not quite sure how you'd look after it. Maybe you'd vacuum it once a week. And as for Pamela, well her and Mum have never got along." Ellie pressed the button for the elevator.

"You're willing for me to drop in now," Heather said.

Ellie shrugged. "If you want. I'm never home on weekends, but any weekday I'm usually about. I like to get all my homework and assignments out of the way during the week so I can spend the weekends with my friends. That's the deal, isn't it Mum?"

"Schooling's important." Sharon entered the elevator when the doors opened.

Ellie pressed the button for the ground floor. "So, are you coming over? I've got homemade vanilla slice made fresh this morning before I went to school." Ellie knew Sam wouldn't mind her taking credit for his cooking. "And a lasagne ready to pop in the oven."

"Homemade as well I suppose," Heather said dryly.

Ellie nodded. "Of course. You're welcome to stay for dinner. It's quite a large lasagne." Mainly because Sam wanted to make sure they had something decent to eat for at least a couple of days.

"This I have got to see," Heather said. "I've been told by several people that you can't cook."

Ellie shrugged. "Some people are better at teaching than others." She smiled. "We'll meet you over there." Ellie stepped out of the elevator and waited for her mum to exit. "You remember where we live, don't you?" She barely managed to keep the sarcasm from her voice.

"I've been there enough times I could find it in my sleep."

"I'm sorry you've wasted so much time trying to catch up with me. I was staying with friends."

"So you said."

Ellie saw Tom's car and almost shouted with relief. "There's our ride. I'll see you soon." She held the back door open for Sharon and waited for her to hop in. She smiled before she got in the car herself. "I'm glad we finally caught up." Ellie held her smile in place until they'd driven away.

"What was that all about?" Tom asked.

"Bloody interfering government worker. You were brilliant, Ellie. Although I don't know how you're going to come up with all those things you said before she arrives." Sharon shook her head. "You didn't have to go overboard. She mightn't have bothered coming if you hadn't been so obvious."

Ellie grinned. "But we do have all those things."

"Not bloody likely. I don't even know if the oven works."

"Yep. It does."

Sharon stared at her for a moment. "What's been going on while I've been stuck in that place? Who taught you how to cook those things?"

"No one. But she's not going to know who cooked them. It's not like they've been signed by the artist."

Sharon chuckled. "I don't think there's a single ounce of your father in you, Ellie. Which is good. A more boring man I couldn't imagine. I still have no idea how I ended up married to him for so long."

Ellie turned to Tom who still looked confused. "Heather's meeting us at our place. Can you unlock my bedroom door and throw the padlock in the top drawer of my duchess? And there's a coffee table in Mum's room that'll need a quick wipe over and two large cushions in my room that can be put in the dining room. We can say we like to eat oriental style or something. And put the lasagne in the oven and make coffee."

"Still plotting and planning, Ellie?" Tom took the keys she gave him, dropping them on his lap before he returned his hand to the steering wheel.

"Always. I'll try and stall her as long as possible. Oh, and I'm not sure if I made Mum's bed."

"Sounds like I'll be doing all the work. What'll you be doing while I'm slaving away?"

"Barricading the front door for as long as possible. Good thing we bought groceries before we picked Mum up. Oh, and can you take the groceries out of the wardrobe in my room? I don't know what she's likely to poke her nose into."

Tom pulled up in front of the house. "No problems, Lisbeth."

Ellie grinned. "Oh I don't know. Lizzie maybe. I don't think I'd say Lisbeth quite yet." She hopped out of the car and walked around to help Sharon out.

"I'm guessing that's a private joke," Sharon said.

Ellie nodded. "Yep."

Sharon watched as Tom went ahead of them to open up the house. "You really like that boy, don't you?"

Ellie nodded. "Yeah."

"Other than Lauren I've never met any of your friends. Why's that, Ellie?"

Ellie shrugged. "I don't have many close friends."

Sharon looked at her a moment longer before she started up the path to the front door. Ellie stood by the car for a minute, watching her mum. What was she meant to say? That she was worried what her friends might see? That she didn't want to risk bringing someone home to find her mum completely and utterly drunk and passed out in the kitchen. It was bad enough Lauren had seen. She didn't think many other people would be as understanding.

Ellie hurried inside and settled Sharon on the sofa. She put her mum's bag in her bedroom and quickly made the bed while she was in there. Then she returned to Sharon.

"Get me a drink, Ellie?"

"Once Heather's gone."

"Drinking isn't a crime," Sharon snapped.

"Yeah, but we don't want to give her any excuses to return, do we?" Ellie turned towards Tom who was bringing the pillows out of her room. "How are you doing for time?"

"Ten minutes would be good."

Ellie nodded. "I'm guessing that's her pulling up now. I'll see how long I can stall her." Ellie hurried outside and met Heather at the front gate. She gestured towards the yard and smiled wryly. "I did tell you we aren't much for gardening. I really can't see why some people are so into it."

"I live in an apartment." Heather shrugged. "I wouldn't have the time to look after a garden either."

No, because you're too busy interfering in other people's lives. Ellie kept her smile in place and her expression neutral. "It took us ages to find this place. Everywhere else we looked had huge yards. I know that's what most people looking for a house want, but we just didn't want to be in our neighbours' pockets like you are in an apartment."

"Are we going to stand out the front all afternoon? We're rapidly losing light," Heather said.

"Of course. Sorry. Terrible manners. I guess I'm just so happy to have Mum home that I'm not thinking right." She leaned in close and lowered her voice. "I'd never tell my friends this because it's really uncool, but I missed Mum. We're close. But I guess that's to be expected since it's only the two of us."

"You aren't trying to stall me, are you?"

Ellie laughed. "Of course not. I just didn't want to say that in front of Tom. No one admits to getting along with their parents. It's just not done."

"Elizabeth–"

Ellie held her hands up. "Sorry. I know. I talk too much. Come on. Let's go inside. I asked Tom if he'd throw the kettle on for me. If we're lucky he might even have made the coffee." She slowly walked towards the front door, avoiding the loose floorboard. Had she given him enough time? Her knees nearly gave out on her when she stepped inside and saw the four side plates with a vanilla slice on each, cups of coffee sitting with them. She glanced at Heather and caught a quick look of surprise before it was masked.

The next half hour crawled by for Ellie. Heather was a difficult woman to convince that everything was normal. Ellie was glad when she declined joining them for dinner, but she wasn't surprised Heather had peeked in the oven to confirm it was homemade lasagne. She owed Sam big time.

Ellie saw Heather out, stopping on the verandah.

"Why would your father be so concerned about you living with your mother? Both he and your stepmother are highly concerned about the situation.

Everything he said was confirmed by the earlier reports I read about your circumstances."

"Oh he's still living in the past. Either that or he can't believe Mum's managed to get her life sorted out, without his help. He was onto her for years. I guess she just needed him out of her life to be able to change it."

Heather nodded. "Possibly." She paused. "If the situation does change, you have my card. I'm here to help."

Ellie nodded and watched as Heather headed towards her car. She returned inside, relieved to have that drama sorted out.

"Now can I have a drink?" Sharon demanded when they heard Heather's car drive away.

"Sure. I'll grab a beer out of the fridge for you, Mum."

Tom, who was in the kitchen, opened a bottle and handed it to her. She smiled at him in thanks before she took the beer to Sharon. Returning to the kitchen, she wrapped her arms around him.

"We've got half an hour before dinner's ready. You want to listen to some music in my room," Ellie asked.

Sharon snorted. "Is that what they're calling it these days?"

Ellie ignored her mum and let Tom go so she could take his hand and lead him to her room. She imagined the next few days were going to be difficult. Either that or she'd be sent out to buy half a dozen bottles of spirits so her mum could work on forgetting all her problems. She wasn't sure which was the worst scenario.

Ellie was slightly out in her guess as to what would happen. After dinner Sharon asked Tom to give her a lift to the drive thru bottle shop where she bought the bottles of spirits herself and then locked herself in her bedroom. Tom stared at Ellie in concern.

"Will you be okay?"

Ellie nodded. "Yeah. She missed two binges. She's working on making up for it."

"Is she likely to invite anyone over?"

"I doubt it. When she's feeling miserable she doesn't like company."

"I feel like a bastard leaving you to deal with this."

"You're not. There's nothing either of us can do. I'll be okay. And you've got an early morning ahead of you." Ellie leaned forward to kiss him.

"I can stay if you want me to."

Ellie shook her head. "Nah. On my little bed? There's barely enough space for one person let alone two."

"Sounds cosy."

Ellie laughed. "Typical."

Tom smiled fleetingly. "Call me if you need me. I don't care what hour or what the reason is."

"Okay. But I can–"

Tom pressed his fingers to her lips. "Try again. This time you stop at okay. Got it?" When Ellie nodded he moved his fingers. "Call if you need me."

Ellie smiled, drawing the word out. "Okay." Tom kissed her until she clung to him, wishing she hadn't told him to leave. She reluctantly let him go when he pulled away.

"I'll see you in the morning."

Ellie nodded. "Night."

"Sweet dreams, Beth." Tom strode to the door and let himself out.

Ellie locked the door and listened as his car drove off. She looked at her mum's bedroom door and sighed. Nothing she could do. She might as well get ready for bed.

Chapter Twenty-Eight

A loud crash woke Ellie from a deep sleep. She stumbled out of bed, unlocking her room. The lounge room light was on but no one was in there. She heard swearing in her mum's room. She hesitated and then knocked on the door. More swearing. She swung the door open and saw her mum on the floor, trying to pull herself up onto the bed.

"Give me your hand, Mum." Ellie pulled her up and turned her so she landed on the bed.

"What would I do without you, Ellie?" Sharon's words were slow and slightly slurred.

"You'd manage. Did you want something?"

"Bottle's empty." Sharon pointed to the bottle lying on the floor. "Need another one."

Ellie nodded and headed for the kitchen without a word. She picked up one of the three bottles left on the bench. She stood there holding it for a moment, trying to get a grip on her emotions. "Suck it up. Some people have it far worse," Ellie muttered. She forced herself to return to her mum's room.

Sharon took a swig from the bottle, patting the bed beside her. "What would I do without you, Ellie?"

Ellie reluctantly sat on the bed. "Are you all right now? It's late. I should head back to bed."

"I don't deserve you, you know." Sharon threw an arm around Ellie and hugged her awkwardly, the smell of alcohol surrounding her.

"Sure you do, Mum."

Sharon shook her head and had another drink. "I'm a terrible mum. Stupid Bitch would be a better mother to you."

Ellie smiled slightly. "The doctor warned you alcohol doesn't mix well with your pain killers. I think it's messed up your mind in a big way. Pamela wishes I was never born."

Sharon patted her on the cheek. "What would I do without you, Ellie?"

Ellie sighed and rose to her feet. "I'm going back to bed."

"I've got money for you, Ellie."

"That's nice, Mum."

"For when you start uni. Your father's paying for

it, but I wanted you to have some so you could enjoy yourself."

"Okay, Mum. Why don't you get some sleep? Have you had any yet?"

"It's in the bottom drawer. Go on, get it out." Sharon pointed to the chest of drawers beside her bed.

"Okay." Ellie knew it was best to humour her mum when she was in this type of mood. "But then you should get some sleep." She opened the drawer and saw the unopened envelopes addressed to her at a post office box.

"Don't tell your father, okay? He'll try and get out of paying."

Ellie took the envelope off the top and opened it up. "Mum! There's a fortune in this account."

"I know you won't touch it until it's time. Just wanted you to know about it. In case something happened to me."

Ellie dropped the statement back in the drawer, closing it. She sat on the bed with her mum again. "Nothing's going to happen to you." She wouldn't let it.

"When I was falling down those stairs I thought I was going to die. All I could think was, I didn't want Stupid Bitch to turn you into her clone. I'm the worst mum."

"No you're not. Becoming her clone would be a fate worse than death. Any decent mum would be concerned about it." Ellie forced herself to smile.

"What would I do without you, Ellie?"

"Go to sleep, Mum. You'll feel better after you have some sleep."

"You remember me getting you to sign some forms because I was going to open you a bank account?"

Ellie nodded. It must have been a few years ago. She'd thought her mum had forgotten all about it. That it was yet another idea that had died before it had barely lived.

"I've been getting money directly deposited into it. Even I can't drink every cent I earn."

"I never thought that." Okay, so maybe she had. But she wasn't about to admit it to her mum when she was in this kind of mood.

"I probably would if it was left in there. I'm sorry, Ellie. I've screwed your life up in a big way, haven't I?"

"Only your life, Mum. I'm keeping mine on track."

"You shouldn't have to."

Ellie shrugged. "I like to."

"What would I do without you, Ellie?"

She rose to her feet again. "Get some sleep, Mum." She dropped a kiss on Sharon's forehead.

Once she was back in her room, Ellie leaned against her closed bedroom door. Well that had been unexpected. Not the apologies. She heard them often enough. A few hours sleep and her mum would forget all about them. The money was what had surprised her. Setting up the account must have been one of the few things her mum had managed to finish in her life. Other than a bottle that was.

Ellie sighed and locked her door. She dropped onto her bed, glancing at the time. Half past four. She was never going to get back to sleep now. She smiled, picking up her phone to send a text to Tom. *Where are you? I'm waiting. Are we still going to the pool this morning?*

She laughed when she read the text he sent back. *Who's this?*

I thought a momentous occasion like this would be something you'd remember.

Is this Lisbeth? Stop toying with me. Return Ellie.

I'm holding her for ransom. You going to rescue her? –Lisbeth

I'll be there in 20.

Ellie quickly dressed, putting her bikini on under her clothes. She grabbed her school uniform and bag then headed for the kitchen. By the time Tom arrived, she'd organised her lunch and eaten breakfast. She met him on the verandah.

Tom kissed her then stared at her for a moment. "Is everything okay?"

Ellie nodded and smiled. "How could it not be? I've just been kissed senseless."

Tom grinned. "Flattery will not distract me."

"You'll be late to the pool."

"We still have plenty of time."

"Can we go?" Ellie pressed her fingers against Tom's lips when it looked like he'd argue. "I promise I'll talk to you later. I've got to get my head around it first."

Tom kissed the fingers that still rested against his lips before he pulled them away. "Before school starts."

Ellie nodded and let him take her schoolbag. She linked her fingers in his and walked beside him to the car. She yawned. It was far too early to be awake. She wouldn't be surprised if she fell asleep during English. Her teacher had a voice that could put a teething baby to sleep.

* * *

That afternoon, Tom pulled up in front of Lauren's house and waited for Lauren and Sam to get out. "Are you sure you'll be fine to get home?"

Sam nodded. "I'll catch a bus. Lauren and I went online and worked out which ones and what time. I can even tie my own shoe laces, brother."

Tom smiled. "It took me so many months to teach you that I'd be devastated if you'd forgotten how."

Sam grinned, brushing his curls out of his eyes before he turned and took Lauren's hand.

As they drove off, Tom glanced at Ellie. "You'll never guess who rang Sam last night."

"Last night? And you're just telling me now? What was wrong with telling me at the pool this morning?"

"I was probably suffering from shock."

"Real funny. Okay, tell me who. I'm no good at twenty questions."

"Only because you don't comprehend the concept that questions are meant to be answered not questioned."

"Dragging this conversation out isn't going to change my mind. You're not coming in when we get to my place. I've got too much schoolwork to get done. No way am I ruining my weekends doing assignments and homework if I can help it."

"It was Michelle. She said a group of them were going to the movies Wednesday night and did he and Lauren want to come along. Then she tacked on the end that I was welcome to come too. Sorry to say, you weren't even mentioned."

Ellie laughed. "She was probably trying to forget I exist. Now what did I tell you? Am I a genius or what?" Her laugh vanished when they pulled up in front of her house to see the front door open and music pouring out. She swore.

"What's going on?" Tom turned off the engine.

"Wait here."

Tom grabbed her arm when she went to open the door. "What's going on, Ellie?"

"Let me go."

"I'm not sitting out here wondering if you're okay. Tell me what's happening." He let go of her arm.

Ellie sighed. It wasn't Tom she was angry at. "Sorry. I think Mum has a few friends over. I hope that's all it is. If she's having a party…" she trailed off. She'd what? She didn't know. "Just give me some time to find out what's happening. If I'm not out in twenty minutes you can come in."

"Don't do anything stupid."

Ellie met his gaze, surprised by the look in his eyes. What did he have to be angry about? She considered asking him, but nodded instead. This time when she opened the car door he didn't try and stop her. She left her schoolbag in the car, striding towards the house. Her lips thinned when she was able to see in the front door. More than a few people. And they'd been there for quite a while by the look of the empty cans and bottles lying around.

"Well, if it isn't little Elizabeth."

Ellie spun towards the bedrooms. Scott stood near her mum's room. She felt like punching the sleazy look off his face. Someone beside her staggered and she took a couple of steps forward so she wasn't knocked over. "What rock did you crawl out from under?"

Scott strode over to her, his smile never faltering. "Don't be like that, Elizabeth. You know I think of you like a daughter. How about a proper greeting, sweet little Elizabeth."

"Good thing you don't have kids. I'd pity any poor bastard who ended up with you as a father." Ellie was pleased to see Scott's smile finally falter. Another person stumbled into her.

They turned around to apologise, then grinned.

"Ellie. Haven't seen you in years. Haven't you grown? Oh, don't that make me feel old."

Ellie nodded. She couldn't think of the woman's name. "Have you seen Mum?"

The woman nodded and pointed to the bedroom. "We came over to cheer her up. Looks like you need cheering instead. What's got you so blue, Ellie? Boy problems?" The woman laughed.

Ellie didn't bother to answer. She strode towards the bedroom. She nearly made it when Scott grabbed her by the arm and turned her to face him. She glared at his hand. "Let me go, or I'll scream."

Scott laughed. "Do you think anyone here'd give a shit? They're all completely plastered."

"Final warning, Scott."

"Or you'll do what?"

Ellie smiled, stepping in close to be able to bring her knee up swiftly and accurately. She grinned when Scott collapsed onto the ground, screaming and swearing. Stepping past him, she entered her mum's room.

Sharon saluted her with a bottle of spirits. There were seven other people in the room with her. One sat on the floor, one on the bed and the others stood about. "Want a drink, Ellie?"

Ellie stared at her mum. Behind her Scott

continued to swear. No one took any notice. Anger rushed through her. She strode over to her mum, ripped the bottle from her hands and threw it against the wall. It shattered, causing the person standing nearby to jump out of the way.

"What was that for?" Sharon frowned. "What a waste."

Tom came to stand beside her. "Are you okay, Ellie?"

Surely it hadn't been twenty minutes already. She nodded, her gaze still on her mum. There were so many words she wanted to speak. She knew it was pointless. Not one word would be remembered tomorrow. The anger that burned in her was a waste of time, but she still couldn't let it go. She turned away and stepped over Scott who now moaned in the doorway. She unlocked her door and held up her hand when Tom would have followed her. "Don't let anyone in." When he nodded, she closed the door and quickly threw a handful of clothes in her overnight bag, including another school uniform. She shoved her laptop in and opened the door. Tom took the bag from her and she shot the barrel bolt home, snapping the padlock on. They walked to the car in silence.

Tom started the car, pulling out onto the street. "What happened to Scott?"

"Someone tried to relocate his testicles."

"You?"

Ellie nodded.

"Where were you aiming to put them?"

"His throat?" When Tom chuckled, Ellie smiled slightly. "I don't think I did a very good job of it though." She sighed and closed her eyes. She felt Tom's hand rest on her thigh and she covered it with her own.

"Are you okay, Ellie?"

"Yeah. I will be."

"You can stay as long as you want."

Ellie opened her eyes. "Thanks. But I'll sort this out. She's not going to party all week too."

"She goes back to work next week, doesn't she?"

Ellie nodded. "Yeah." She closed her eyes again as she frantically thought over all her options. There weren't a lot. The bank statement came to mind. No, she wouldn't touch that unless she was completely desperate. It'd pay for accommodation during the years she'd be at uni. If she needed it to. Although she was sure she could con her father into paying for that. Especially if Pamela thought she'd be visiting every second she could.

"You'll let me know if I can help?"

Ellie nodded, her eyes still closed. She would open them when they reached Tom's house. Until then she was going to pretend the rest of the world didn't exist. Her life was a mess again. Why couldn't things go right for more than a day or two at a time? Not one single thing about this day had gone well. Starting with her mum waking her early in the morning. An image of Scott on the floor brought a smile to her face. Well, maybe something had gone well. Seeing him crumple like that had been extremely satisfying. Go Lisbeth! He better keep his distance because she wasn't putting up with any of his crap ever again.

Chapter Twenty-Nine

The next afternoon Ellie sat in the car with Tom and stared at her house. Most of the day had been a blur. Throughout the day she hadn't been able to stop thinking about what was going on at home. Now she was sitting out the front, she didn't want to go in and find out. She straightened her shoulders. She wasn't the sort to sit about moaning and complaining. Well, not for long anyway. Time to see how screwed up her life currently was.

"You don't have to go in there alone," Tom said.

Ellie nodded. "I do."

"Let me know if everything's okay. I'm not leaving until you tell me it's safe for you in there."

"It will be. It's too quiet to be otherwise."

"Ring me if you need me."

Ellie smiled. "Okay." She said the word with a great deal of exaggeration.

Tom returned her smile. "It looks like you were right. You can teach old dogs new tricks."

Ellie's smile became a grin. "I'll wave to you from the front door if it's okay for you to go."

Tom nodded and then drew her close for a kiss. "Will you be online tonight?"

"Eight?"

"I'll be waiting."

Ellie rested her palm against his face, staring into his eyes for a minute. Some things she couldn't bring herself to voice. A marriage proposal? Not a problem. The words that should have come long before it? Well, they got stuck in her throat. "Thank you," she said softly. She grabbed her bags and raced to the house.

The front door was unlocked. She swung it open and determinedly stepped inside. It was a mess. But other than her mum passed out on the sofa, it was empty. She put her bags in her room, locked it again and opened up all the windows. Yep, empty. She breathed a sigh of relief and went to stand in the front doorway. She waved to Tom who waved at her before he started the car and drove away. Ellie turned back to face her mum.

No point in waiting around for her to wake up.

Might as well get it over with. Ellie moved closer. "Mum." She stirred. "Mum!"

Sharon opened her eyes and stared blearily up at Ellie. "What? Grab me something for this headache and stop shouting."

Ellie waded through the mess and grabbed Panadol off the top of the fridge. She threw them in Sharon's lap. "I'm not impressed."

"What the bloody hell are you going on about? Can't you see I'm trying to sleep?"

"I don't care if you bring the house down around your ears on the weekend. I'd prefer you didn't, but I'm not affected by it."

"So generous of you. Since when do I have to ask your permission?"

Ellie ignored the sarcastic comment. "But I do care if you have one of your drunken parties during the week. I live here too you know."

"It wasn't planned. Scott came over. Things snowballed from there. And what's your problem with him? He told me this morning that you were a complete bitch to him yesterday."

"Really?" Ellie's fists clenched. "Next time he thinks he can put his hands on me I won't bother trying to knee his balls through to his throat, I'll cut them off. And you can tell him that."

"Now Ellie, Scott's harmless. He wouldn't-"

"Stop. I don't want to hear any of your pathetic excuses. You can have whoever you want as your friend. Any pathetic loser who wanders in off the street with a bottle of alcohol for all I care. But I'm not putting up with them."

"What's up your butt?

"This." She indicated the mess with a sweep of her hand. "I won't put up with this during the week."

"Oh go away, Ellie. I'm not in the mood for it."

"Too bad."

"Don't take that tone with me. You're bloody lucky I give you as much freedom as I do. I bet your father wouldn't let you get away with the shit I let you get away with."

"No more parties during the week."

"Or what?"

"I leave." She had to draw the line somewhere.

Sharon laughed. "Yeah right, Ellie. You're bluffing. You know you wouldn't get the same sort of deal at your father's."

"I never once said I'd move in with him. I'd rather live in a foster home first." Okay, so maybe not, but it was an option.

"And I bet they wouldn't let you get away with what I do."

Ellie shrugged. "I didn't say I'd take that option. Aren't you the one who keeps telling me I always land on my feet? Give me a week and I could come up with a dozen options. Do you really want me to leave? Is it such a chore living with me? Is having parties during the week more important to you than having me stay?"

Sharon stared at her. "I actually think you might be serious."

Ellie rolled her eyes. "I know you've tried to kill off every brain cell possible with your drinking, but I didn't think it was that hard a concept to understand."

"Stop being a bitch, Ellie."

"Then stop trying to win worst mother of the year award."

"That was low."

"So is throwing a party in the middle of the week so I had nowhere to stay."

"Next you'll be telling me you had to sleep on some park bench."

"No, I didn't." Ellie stared at Sharon. She decided to bend the truth slightly. She had done it, just not last night. "It was a railway station."

"Stop speaking shit."

"I'm not."

Sharon shook her head.

"I had a bag lady tell me to make myself scarce when the police do their sweep through. She even gave me the hours. Told me who to avoid and offered to share her dinner with me. She even pointed out there was hardly any dirt on it since no one had walked on it when it was dropped on the ground."

"Ellie…"

"No more parties during the week."

Sharon dropped her head into her hands. "Are you going to tell your father?"

"No. This is between you and me."

"You must hate me." Sharon raised her head. Tears streaked her cheeks.

Ellie shook her head. "No." She shrugged. "You're my mum."

"Not much of a one."

"Probably not. But since you're the one I'm stuck with I'm willing to make the best of it."

"So generous of you, Ellie," Sharon said bitterly.

"No. Generous is cleaning this mess up each week." Ellie gestured towards the room. "Generous is buying the groceries and paying the bills and making sure there's always something for you to eat. Correct me if I'm wrong, but isn't that the parent's job?"

"Ellie… I don't… why are you here, Ellie? Why do you put up with me?"

"Because someone has to deal with it all and I know you won't. But I'm not sticking around if I've got to put up with parties during the week. The only thing I'm asking is that from Sunday afternoon to Friday morning none of your friends are welcome here. Ever."

"Don't push it, Ellie. You're being ridiculous."

"Is that your answer? Because if it is, I'll be out of here by Friday."

"And where will you go?"

Ellie stared at her mum, her expression closed. "That would not be your problem." She thought of the money sitting in the account her mum had opened for her. She'd have to take one of those statements so she could go and see the bank. And probably cancel any cards that had been issued for the account. She should also give them a different mailing address too.

"Oh what does it matter? I'm usually working during the week. Fine. But only because it suits me. Not because of your threats. Now leave me alone. My head's killing me." Sharon lay back on the sofa, closing her eyes.

Ellie stared at Sharon for a couple of minutes before she turned away. Heading straight for Sharon's bedroom, she opened the bottom drawer. After some searching through the contents she was surprised to find a keycard and pin number. She took them and the latest statement. She would make sure Sharon couldn't take the money she'd set aside for her. Life felt less uncertain knowing she had some money she could use if it all fell apart again.

Once the keycard and statement were safe in her room, she cleaned up the mess. It wasn't as bad as it was on a Sunday. But she guessed it had only been a single day, not a weekend of partying. The bit that annoyed her most was that she'd have to do this clean up twice in one week.

By the time Ellie got the mess cleaned up, it was nearly eight. Tom was already online waiting for her. She signed in as offline. She didn't think she could face chatting to anyone else right now.

Ellie says: Finally finished.

TW says: How are you?

Ellie says: Fine.

TW says: Seriously?

Ellie says: Don't start.

TW says: So you're not fine.

Ellie's phone started to ring and she stared down at it on the desk. She was tempted to ignore Tom.

When he sent a message telling her to answer the phone, she sighed. She had to give him top points for being persistent. "What?"

"What happened?"

"Nothing."

"Try again."

"Who do you think you are? My therapist?"

"Do I get to lie on the couch with you?"

Ellie couldn't prevent a smile from starting. "Do you ever think of anything else?"

"Yeah. Now do you want to tell me what's wrong?"

"Nothing. I just had a bit of an argument with Mum, that's all."

"Are you sure you want to stay there tonight? I could come and get you."

"What do you want me to do? Move in with you? I can't leave Mum here on her own. Who'd take care of her?"

"Have you thought that maybe that's what she needs?"

Ellie was silent a moment. "Yeah. But not yet. Maybe when I start uni."

"Okay."

Silence fell again until Ellie broke it. "Did I thank you for helping me out with Heather the other day?"

"No."

"Thank you. I guess she brought back bad memories. Every time I saw her I just about had a panic attack."

"You hid it well."

"Is that all you're going to say?"

Tom sighed. "Of course I want to ask you about the bad memories, but I was going to wait until this weekend."

That was the last thing Ellie wanted. It was much easier to spill her secrets over the phone when he wasn't watching her. "I was in foster care when I was five."

"What was it like?"

"I kept asking to go home. And these two strangers kept telling me I was home. They had two older kids of their own. A boy and a girl. I had to share a room with the girl. I had none of my own things with me and she had to share her stuff with me. And her mum kept praising her for being nice to the poor little girl. I didn't need anything of hers. I had my own things. At home. And they wouldn't let me go there."

"Didn't you get to see your parents?"

"Dad shoved Mum in some rehab so they could get me back. She played their little game so she could get out quicker and he was too busy at work to come and see me. I must have tried to run away every day. I didn't know how to get home, but that didn't stop me from trying."

"So you've always been stubborn."

Ellie laughed. "Yeah, I suppose so." She fell silent again. "I remember the day Mum was finally allowed to pick me up. I was sitting by the front door, like I did most days, wearing some stupid frilly dress. I can't remember what colour it was, but I do remember the lace made me feel itchy. She came bursting in the door with some government official and stared at me. Her first words were 'what is that crap she's wearing? How can a kid climb a tree in all those frills?' I just sat there and stared at her. I could hardly believe she'd finally come to get me."

"How long were you there?"

"Two months. But it felt like years."

"What were your foster parents like?"

"They weren't mean or anything. Just strangers. I'd been stolen from my home and shoved with people I didn't even know. I still get the urge to run whenever I see a cop."

Silence fell again. This time it was Tom who broke it. "I really don't know what to say. I guess I feel sorry for that little kid, but not for you. Actually,

I kinda feel sorry for the hoops you made Heather jump through."

Ellie laughed. "I am never going to forget her expression when she realised I'd told her the truth at the hospital."

"Ellie."

"Yeah."

"Thank you for telling me."

"Did I have a choice? You'd have eventually dragged it out of me."

"Only because I love you. It's not just because I'm curious."

She tried. She really did. The words wouldn't come. The feeling was there, had been for ages, but the words were stuck in her throat. "Huh. And I thought it was because of your obsessive behaviour that makes you unable to drop anything."

Tom laughed softly. "Nice try."

"I should let you get some sleep since you get up at a ridiculous hour of the morning."

"Yeah. Night Ellie. Love you."

Once again the words refused to come. Instead, she hung up and turned to her laptop.

Ellie says: Dream of me :)

TW says: Always.

Sighing, she shut down her laptop, and stared at the screen until it went black. She took a deep breath. "Love you." Her words were a whisper. She guessed she could say them. When she was alone. She closed the lid of her laptop as she rose from her desk. Maybe practice would help. She shook her head with a short laugh. Who was she kidding? Those words scared the hell out of her. She already had one person she loved. Someone who relied heavily on her. Did she really need more of that responsibility?

She dropped onto her bed. She knew Tom was nothing like her mum. If anything, he was the one who liked to take care of things. Rationally, she knew that. It was the irrational thoughts that got in the way. Somehow she had to sort them out. She wasn't about to let them screw up one of the best things that had ever happened to her.

Chapter Thirty

Sitting in the near dark, Ellie sent a text message to Lauren as she waited for the laptop to turn on. *Go online immediately.* She smiled when Lauren sent a message back. *Better be good.* Ellie glanced at the bed where Tom was tangled in the sheets, fast asleep. Dim light shone through the window onto him. She was too happy to sleep. Turning back to the laptop, she signed into her messenger.

Ellie says: Hey : D

Waiting for Santa says: Better be real good. I was having a brilliant dream.

Ellie says: Oh it's way good.

Waiting for Santa says: Well….

Ellie says: Remember how we promised to let each other know, as soon as humanly possible, about our very first time with someone?

Waiting for Santa says: No!

Ellie says: Yes!

Waiting for Santa says: We are talking about the same subject.

Ellie says: I hope so : D

Waiting for Santa says: You and Tom?

Ellie says: Yep : D

Waiting for Santa says: Wow! What was it like? Tell me every little detail

Ellie says: No way. Would you tell me every little detail if it was you and Sam?

Waiting for Santa says: Maybe.

Ellie says: Really?

Waiting for Santa says: Okay. But at least tell me what it was like.

Ellie says: Does the fact I can't stop grinning tell you?

Waiting for Santa says: : D

Tom sat up in the bed. "Ellie?"

"One minute."

"What are you doing on my laptop?"

"I'll be there in a minute."

"Hurry up. It's lonely over here."

"I thought you were asleep."

"So you stole my shirt and went online? Are you chatting to Lauren?"

Ellie chuckled. "Maybe."

"You're not telling her are you?" Tom hopped out of bed, coming over to the desk.

Ellie covered the screen with her hands. "You're naked!"

"So were you. Show me what you told her."

Ellie reluctantly moved her hands away.

Waiting for Santa says: You still there? You've gone real quiet.

Waiting for Santa says: Hello?

Waiting for Santa says: If you don't answer soon I'm going back to bed.

Ellie says: Sorry. Tom just woke up. He's reading what I told you *rolls eyes* As if his ego isn't bad enough already.

Waiting for Santa says: Hi Tom : D

Ellie says: He said hi and Merry Christmas.

Waiting for Santa says: Hey, yeah, it's after midnight.

Waiting for Santa says: Merry Christmas you pair.

Ellie says: I'll let you get back to sleep. And see you for lunch tomorrow. You sure your parents are happy to join us over here.

Waiting for Santa says: Happy! Any happier and I think Mum'd explode. She's been telling all her friends she's having a Christmas dinner cooked by The Gregory. And the way she says it you'd swear it's in capital letters.

Ellie says: lol. I'll see you then. I'll let you get back to sleep.

Waiting for Santa says: K. But first I'm going to send Sam a Merry Christmas text : D

Ellie says: lol. I'm sure he'll appreciate it ;)

Waiting for Santa says: Bibi.

Ellie says: Buh-bye.

Ellie turned off the laptop and rose to her feet. She was still grinning when Tom wrapped his arms around her. "Merry Christmas."

Tom kissed her. "Merry Christmas. So, still grinning hey?"

Ellie shook her head. "I knew I should have exited the window before you read it. You'll be insufferable now."

"Come back to bed and we'll see if I can keep you grinning."

"Ego!"

Tom laughed. "Not at all. A statement of truth."

Ellie walked back to the bed with him and paused

beside it. Even with the light coming through the window, his face was mostly shadows, but she couldn't miss seeing his smile. "I'm glad Lauren's mum caught us sneaking back in that night so I had to find somewhere else to stay on weekends."

"Why did you make yourself up to look like Frankenstein's Bride?"

"Because the last guy I went home with thought I was agreeing to far more than somewhere to crash for the night."

"You didn't need the outfit. Sam and I know what the word no means."

"I know that now, but I didn't at the time." She smiled. "But I must say, I think I'm going to miss Frankie."

"Too bad. Frankie can't have you back."

"Why's that?"

"Because I love you and would be devastated if you left."

"Even with all the crap in my life?"

"I barely notice it."

Ellie laughed. "Well, I suppose love is blind."

"And what makes you say that?"

"Personal experience?"

"And what personal experience would that be?"

Ellie smiled and let the silence drag out for a

moment. She knew this time she could say the words, but she wanted to draw the moment out. To savour it. "I love you too."

Tom grinned just before his lips met hers. He eventually drew back, still smiling. "I know. But it's nice to hear."

Ellie forced herself to look serious. "Now what was all that bragging about you keeping me grinning? I don't seem to be grinning anymore."

"Hmm, it seems like you could be right. Guess I'd better fix that."

Ellie squealed as Tom caused her to lose her balance and land on the bed. He landed beside her. She grinned as she stared at him. Who'd have thought spending a weekend looking like an ugly stepsister could change everything so much? Life was always so full of surprises. Tom's lips met hers and thinking became an effort. This was the best Christmas ever. She couldn't wait to see what the New Year would bring.

Free Ebook

Subscribe to Avril's newsletter to receive a free ebook. This ebook is exclusive to those on her mailing list. To find out more about this offer visit: http://www.avrilsabine.com/free-ebook/

*

We value your privacy and will not sell, rent, exchange or loan your email address to third parties. Your information is confidential and you are under no obligation to remain on the mailing list and can unsubscribe at any time.

Acknowledgements

Thanks to the usual crew. Are you getting tired of me thanking you yet? I hope not because I couldn't manage without you.

To The Reader

If you enjoyed this book, why not consider leaving a review to help other readers discover it too? Reader engagement is one of the few ways that lets an author know readers want more books in a particular series or genre. So leave a review and tell friends, not only about this book but also about other ones you've enjoyed, so you can continue to enjoy books by your favourite authors for years to come.

Dreams are meant to be lived,

Avril.

About The Author

Avril is an Australian author who lives with her family on acreage in South East Queensland. She writes mostly young adult speculative fiction, but has been known to dabble in other genres. You can find more information about her at her website www.avrilsabine.com where you can also subscribe to her newsletter to be kept informed about new releases, current projects, blog posts and exclusive news.

Titles By Avril Sabine

Stories about strong characters and characters who discover their strengths.

SERIES

Assassins Of The Dead- Young Adult Fantasy/ Paranormal

Book 1: Dark Blade

Book 2: Dragon Touched

Book 3: Society Against Vampires

Book 4: King's Request

Dragon Blood- Young Adult Urban Fantasy (with elements of romance)

(5 book series)

Book 1: Pliethin

Book 2: Wyvern

Book 3: Surety

Book 4: Knight

Book 5: Mage

Dragon Mage- Young Adult Urban Fantasy (with elements of romance)

(Series two of Dragon Blood series)

Book 1: Promise

Dragon Blood Chronicles- Young Adult Urban Fantasy (with elements of romance)

(Companion stand alone series to Dragon Blood)

Book 1: Oath

Book 2: Betrayed

Guardians Of The Round Table- Young Adult Fantasy LitRPG

(Co-written with Storm and Rhys Petersen)

Book 1: Dexterity Fail

Book 2: Goblin Boots

Book 3: Singed Feathers

Book 4: Frog Mage

Book 5: Crystal Mine

Book 6: Cursed Harp

Rosie's Rangers- Young Adult Western Steampunk

(6 book series)

Book 1: Justice

Book 2: Vengeance

Book 3: Treachery

Book 4: Accused

Book 5: Wanted

Book 6: Corruption

Mark Of Kings- Children's Fantasy

(Upper middle grade/preteen)

(4 book series)

Book 1: The Arena

Book 2: The Island

Book 3: The Assassin

Book 4: The King

STAND ALONE SERIES

*Demon Hunters- Young Adult Urban Fantasy/
Horror (with elements of romance)*

Book 1: Blood Sacrifice

Book 2: Retribution

Book 3: Tainted

Book 4: Premonition

Book 5: Cursed

Book 6: Feud

Book 7: Extrication

Plea Of The Damned- Young Adult Urban Fantasy/Paranormal

(6 book series)

Book 1: Forgive Me Lucy

Book 2: Forgive Me Aiden

Book 3: Forgive Me Jena

Book 4: Forgive Me Kobe

Book 5: Forgive Me Marti

Book 6: Forgive Me Dawson

Realms Of The Fae- Young Adult Urban Fantasy (with elements of romance)

The Sword (short story in Like A Girl Anthology)

Heart Of Stone

Book 1: A Debt Owed

Book 2: Marked By The Hunt

Book 3: The Magic Collector

Book 4: An Unexpected Betrayal

Book 5: Imprisoned By Iron

Fairytales Retold (Short Stories)

Snow-White And Rose-Red

The Twelve Brothers

The Light Princess

Beauty And The Beast

Sleeping Beauty

Aschenputtel

The Golden Bird

The Frog Prince

The Death Of Koshchei The Deathless

Myths And Legends Retold (Short Stories)

Ion, Son Of Apollo

Sir Gawain And The Maid With The Narrow Sleeves

Princess Ilse, The Giant's Daughter

YOUNG ADULT NOVELS

Young Adult Fantasy (with elements of romance)

Elf Sight

Earth Bound

Young Adult Urban Fantasy

Stone Warrior (with elements of romance)

The Jungle Inside

Young Adult Contemporary (with elements of romance)

Through Your Eyes

The Ugly Stepsister

Perfect Little Princess

Young Adult Contemporary/Paranormal

Whispers In The Dark (with elements of romance and same sex relationships)

Over Too Soon (with elements of romance)

Young Adult Sci-Fi

Experiment X-One-Six (Urban Sci-Fi/Superheroes)

An Endless Dawn (Post Apocalyptic Sci-Fi)

CHILDREN'S BOOKS

Dragon Lord (Preteen/early teens) (Fantasy)

The Irish Wizard (Upper middle grade) (Urban Fantasy)

SHORT STORIES

Urban Fantasy

Eternally Late

Dealings With Joe

Glimpses (short story in That Moment When Anthology)

Contemporary

The Brat Next Door

Fantasy LitRPG

(Set in the same world as Guardians Of The Round Table Series)

Tales Of Inadon 1: The Disc (Co-written with Storm and Rhys Petersen) (short story in Game On! Anthology)

Post Apocalyptic Sci-Fi

Compulsive Directive

NONFICTION

A Year Of Weekly Writing Exercises (Creative Writing)

Cooking For Families With Allergies (Cooking) (Co-written with Storm Petersen)

Tell Me A Story, Grandma (Memoir)

For the most up to date details on available titles visit:

www.avrilsabine.com/books/bibliography

Disclaimer

This is a work of fiction. Names, characters, businesses, places, events and incidents are either the products of the author's imagination or used in a fictitious manner. Any resemblance to actual persons, living or dead, or actual events is purely coincidental. The opinions expressed or beliefs held are those of the characters and should not be assumed to be the opinions or beliefs of the author.

www.ingramcontent.com/pod-product-compliance
Lightning Source LLC
Chambersburg PA
CBHW050747190726
48285CB00005B/1568